# *The Time Machine*

## H. G. WELLS

Level 4

Retold by David Maule
Series Editors: Andy Hopkins and Jocelyn Potter

D1501659

**Pearson Education Limited**
Edinburgh Gate, Harlow,
Essex CM20 2JE, England
and Associated Companies throughout the world.

ISBN 978-1-4058-8234-7

First published 2006
This edition published 2008

5 7 9 10 8 6

Typeset by Graphicraft Limited, Hong Kong
Set in 11/14pt Bembo
Printed in China
SWTC/05

Produced for the Publishers by
Graphicraft Productions Limited, Dartford, UK

Published by Pearson Education Limited in association with
Penguin Books Ltd, both companies being subsidiaries of Pearson Plc

For a complete list of the titles available in the Penguin Readers series please write to your local
Pearson Education office or to: Penguin Readers Marketing Department, Pearson Education,
Edinburgh Gate, Harlow, Essex, CM20 2JE

# Contents

# Introduction

*'When I had started building the Time Machine, I had had the stupid idea that the people of the future would certainly be far ahead of us in all their inventions.'*

The most important person in this book – we know him only as the Time Traveller – has built his own time machine and has gone forwards into the future, to the year 802,701. He expects to find a world with more intelligent people, better machines and a much better way of living. Perhaps we expect this too, because most books and films about time travel show the future in this way.

Instead, he discovers a world where people live simple lives. They play and dance in the sunshine. They sleep in groups in large ruined buildings from an earlier time. They eat nothing except fruit and own nothing except the clothes they wear. At first this is only inconvenient for the Time Traveller, because he has come badly-prepared for a world like this. He has brought only a box of matches. He has no camera, no medicine, not even anything to smoke. To us, a world without meat or tobacco may seem better, or at least healthier, than the modern world, but HG Wells wrote this book at the end of the nineteenth century. At that time people ate meat if they could afford it, and most men smoked, and very few people really questioned these habits.

During the 1800s, the lives of people in Britain had changed more than they ever had before. A hundred years earlier, most had worked on the land and had lived very similar lives to the lives of their parents. By 1895, when *The Time Machine* appeared, millions had moved to the growing cities and were working in factories. The richer people were able to enjoy the things that the new machines produced. But life for the ordinary workers and their families was difficult, dirty and often dangerous.

The future of the great numbers of workers in the cities, and of society in general, was on many people's minds. It was not really surprising that Karl Marx had lived in London. He had seen the situation of the workers there and put the results of his thinking into his books. Wells was not a follower of Marx, but he believed that everybody should have the chance to go to school, that science could improve people's lives and that a better, fairer kind of society was possible.

At the beginning of the book, Wells shows us that the Time Traveller lives in a large house and has servants. His friends include a doctor, a psychologist and the editor of a newspaper – people who have good jobs. The Time Traveller seems to do no regular work himself, so either he has a lot of money or he makes money from his inventions. Wells then sends him forwards in time to a possible future. In this time the workers and the managers have become more and more separate, until they have almost lost contact with each other completely. Their different lives have changed them into physically quite different species. The workers are ugly creatures who live almost like animals, although they still remember how to make things, while the managers have changed into people who are small, quite beautiful – and completely useless.

It is possible to see this as the old fight between good and bad, but Wells was not a very religious man. Also, to help the beautiful people, the Time Traveller is ready to fight against the others. On a number of occasions he attacks those in the other group, and can only with difficulty stop himself killing them. This is perhaps not the normal behaviour of a 'good' man, but the end of the nineteenth century was a time when war, often fought in colourful uniforms, was still seen as an activity in which men showed that they were men. Nobody could imagine the great killing of the next fifty years. In the book, Wells says that difficulties and dangers make people strong, clever and intelligent, and it is clear that strength includes the ability and willingness to fight. Wells argued for world peace but understood the nature of man. So when he uses weapons, the Time Traveller only does what was expected of a man of his time. But he can dance too, and when he fights or when he dances he shows types of behaviour that belong to each of the two human groups of the future.

One of the dinner guests in Chapter 1 is a psychologist. Like many people of his time, Wells was interested in this new science and it is also possible to see the two social groups of the future as different parts of the human mind. Sigmund Freud's first book appeared in the same year as *The Time Machine*, and Robert Louis Stevenson's *The Strange Case of Dr Jekyll and Mr Hyde* (also a Penguin Reader) had come out less than ten years before. In that book, Stevenson used science to separate the good and bad sides of the same person. In a different way, Wells was doing something similar.

Wells was, perhaps, also examining his own behaviour. He was a very hard worker. In his life he wrote more than Dickens and Shakespeare together. But he also enjoyed his free time – sometimes in a way that shocked many people. Although Wells married his cousin in 1891, just over a year later he ran away with – and later married – one of his students. Later, he had a great number of relationships with other women, which his wife appeared to accept.

When the Time Traveller goes into the future, he meets a woman called Weena and they become close friends. We are told that Weena, like the others of her group, is small and almost childlike. To us, there may be something slightly worrying about this description, but confident women with ideas of equality were unusual in Wells's time. Some existed: they were known as New Women, and in his book *Ann Veronica* (1909) Wells wrote about one of them. But in general, middle-class women were seen as weak creatures to be protected by men. And so the Time Traveller protects Weena, and she cares for him. Nothing more happens in the relationship between them. This book is not a love story.

At times in the book we may feel that all the human work of Wells's time, all the scientific progress, has been useless in the end. Wells left his course at a London science college before he finished it because he had lost interest in his studies. At one point the Time Traveller sees some old books that have fallen to pieces. He thinks about the scientific papers he wrote himself, which have now turned to dust.

After he leaves the year 802,701 the Time Traveller travels forwards, further and further in time, until he finally stops his machine on a frozen beach under an enormous red dying sun. The world has stopped turning and its end is near. In the end the power of nature is greater than the power of science, and there is no real purpose to human life. This sadness in the book may be the result of the mood of the time. The story was written at the very end of the 1800s, when many people were afraid of the new century. Some felt – correctly – that a great war between European countries was coming, and that things would never be the same again. But it may be that Wells could see beyond the daily lives of people, with their hopes and fears, beyond life and death, to a greater picture in which all of us simply live in this world and, one day, will leave it.

HG Wells wrote about the ideas and problems of his time, but he also wrote about feelings which are true in any time, including our own. That is one reason why *The Time Machine*, like a number of his other books, is still popular today.

Herbert George Wells was born in England in 1866. He did not come from a rich family. His parents had a small shop but it was not successful and closed when he was thirteen. He worked at different times in a clothes shop and a chemist's. He always read a lot and later managed to get a place at a science college. After he left there he became a teacher, but he was badly hurt while playing football and this meant that he could not continue. He then worked in London, writing for newspapers and doing some teaching of small groups. None of this made him much money.

*The Time Machine* was his first fictional work. It appeared in weekly parts in a magazine in 1894 and as a book the following year. At the time, Wells was married to his second wife and was trying to support both her and her mother. He needed to make money, so he wrote it quite quickly. Although he was never really happy with the finished book, it was a great success and allowed him to continue as a writer.

It is not easy for us to understand how different this book was from others of the time. It is the first real science fiction book. It introduces the reader to the idea of time as the fourth dimension, with the three dimensions of space, ten years before Einstein made it part of scientific thinking. Wells also describes a simple mechanical answer to the problem of time travel – a time machine. Nobody had ever described time travel in a machine before, and the words 'time machine' entered the English language.

After the great success of this book, Wells wrote more science fiction. His most famous books are *The Island of Dr Moreau* (1896), *The Invisible Man* (1897), *The War of the Worlds* (1898) and *The First Men in the Moon* (1901). All of them have been filmed, some more than once. *The War of the Worlds* and *The Invisible Man* are also Penguin Readers. HG Wells died in London in 1946.

'This line shows the changes in temperature.'

## Chapter 1    The Time Traveller

The Time Traveller (it will be convenient to call him this) was talking to us about geometry. His grey eyes shone and his usually pale face was red and excited. The fire burned brightly and there was that relaxed after-dinner feeling when thoughts run freely.

'You must listen carefully. I shall have to destroy one or two ideas that almost everyone accepts – for example, the geometry that they taught you at school. You know, of course, that a mathematical line, a line with no thickness, doesn't really exist. They taught you that? A mathematical model, which only has length, width and thickness, doesn't really exist either. It's just an idea.'

'That's all right,' said the Psychologist.

'But if you make that model out of a material,' said Filby, a red-haired man who liked an argument, 'it exists. All real things exist.'

'Most people think so. But wait a moment. Imagine a thing that doesn't last for any time. Can it have a real existence?' Filby looked thoughtful. 'Clearly,' the Time Traveller said, 'a real body must have length, width, thickness (the dimensions of space) – and also exist in time. But through a natural human weakness, we usually forget the fourth of these.'

'That,' said a very young man, 'is very clear.'

'Well, I don't mind telling you that I have been at work on this geometry of four dimensions for some time. Some of my results are interesting. Here is a record of the weather. This line shows the changes in temperature. Yesterday it was quite high, last night it fell, then this morning it rose again. Surely that line is not in any of the dimensions of space that we generally understand? It is along the time-dimension.'

'But,' said the Medical Man, looking hard at the fire, 'if time is really only a fourth dimension of space, why can't we move about in it as we move in the other dimensions?'

The Time Traveller smiled. 'Are you so sure we can move freely in space? We can go right and left, backwards and forwards freely enough. But up and down? That isn't so easy.'

'Well, we can move a little up and down,' said the Medical Man. 'But we can't move at all in time. We are always in the present moment.'

'That is at the centre of my great discovery. Why can a modern man not hope that one day he might travel in time?'

'It doesn't make sense,' said Filby.

'Possibly not,' said the Time Traveller. 'But now you begin to see the reason for my work on the geometry of four dimensions. Long ago I had an idea for a machine that can travel in any direction of space and time, as the driver wants.'

Filby started to laugh.

'But I have proved this by experiment,' said the Time Traveller.

'It would be very useful for the historian,' the Psychologist suggested. 'He could travel back and see how things really happened!'

'Then there is the future,' said the Very Young Man. 'Just think! You could put all your money in the bank, leave it to grow and hurry on ahead!'

'To discover a society,' I said, 'that doesn't use money.'

'Of all the crazy ideas!' began the Psychologist.

'It seemed so to me, and I never talked about it until –'

'An experiment!' I cried. 'You are going to prove *that*?'

'Let's see what you can do,' said the Psychologist, 'though I think it's all rubbish.'

The Time Traveller smiled at us. Then, with his hands deep inside his trouser pockets, he walked slowly out of the room and we heard him going down to the laboratory.

The Psychologist looked at us. 'I wonder what he's got?'

'A trick probably,' said the Medical Man, and Filby tried to tell us about a trick he had seen once, but before he had really started his story the Time Traveller came back.

He held something in his hand. It was made of shiny metal and was not much larger than a small clock. And now I must be exact, because unless you believe his explanation it is impossible to explain what happened next.

He took one of the small tables in the room and put it in front of the fire. On this he placed the machine. Then he placed a chair next to it and sat down. The only other object on the table was a small lamp, the light of which fell on the model.

I sat in a low chair nearest the fire and I pulled this forwards so I was almost between the Time Traveller and the fire. Filby sat behind him, looking over his shoulder. The Medical Man watched him from the right; the Psychologist from the left. The Very Young Man stood behind the Psychologist. We were all wide awake. I cannot believe that a trick was played on us under these conditions.

'This little thing,' said the Time Traveller, resting his elbows on the table and pressing his hands together above the machine, 'is only a model. It is my plan for a machine to travel through time. You will notice that it looks a little rough, and this bar has an odd shining appearance – it looks quite unreal.' He pointed to this part with his finger. 'Also, here is one little white lever, and here is another.'

The Medical Man got out of his chair and looked closely into the thing. 'It's beautifully made,' he said.

'It took two years to make,' said the Time Traveller. Then, when we had all had a close look, he said, 'Now I want you to understand clearly that this lever sends the machine flying into the future, and this other one sends it into the past.

'Soon, I'm going to press the lever and the machine will disappear into future time. Have a good look at the thing. Look at the table too, and satisfy yourself that there can be no tricks. I don't want to waste this model and then be told I'm dishonest.'

There was a minute's pause perhaps. The Psychologist opened his mouth to speak to me but closed it again. Then the Time Traveller put out his finger towards the lever.

'No,' he said suddenly, pulling his finger away again. 'Lend me your hand.' And turning to the Psychologist, he took that person's hand in his own and told him to put out his first finger and touch the lever.

So the Psychologist himself sent the model time machine on its endless journey. We all saw the lever turn. I am completely certain there was no trick. There was a breath of wind and the lamp flame jumped. The machine suddenly turned round, looked unclear, was seen like a ghost for a second and was gone – disappeared! Except for the lamp, the table was empty.

Everyone was silent for a minute. Then the Psychologist recovered from his surprise and looked under the table.

The Time Traveller laughed cheerfully. 'Well?' he said.

We all stared.

'My friend,' said the Medical Man quietly, 'are you serious about this? Do you really believe that machine has travelled in time?'

'Certainly,' said the Time Traveller. 'And I have a big machine nearly finished in there' – he pointed to the laboratory – 'and when that is put together I intend to go on a journey myself.'

'You mean to say that that machine has travelled into the future?' said Filby.

'Into the future or the past – I'm not completely sure which.'

After some time the Psychologist said, 'It has gone into the past if it has gone anywhere.'

'Why?' said the Time Traveller.

'Because I'm quite sure that it hasn't moved in space, and if it travelled into the future it would still be here all this time. It would have to travel through the time that is passing as we stand here.'

'But,' I said, 'if it travelled into the past, why wasn't it here when we first came into this room, and last Thursday when we were here – and the Thursday before that?'

'Let's be fair – these are serious questions,' said Filby, turning towards the Time Traveller.

'That can be explained,' the Time Traveller said to the Psychologist. 'It's there but can't be seen.'

'Of course,' said the Psychologist. 'That's simple enough. Why didn't I think of it? We can't see it, in the same way that we can't see a bullet flying through the air. If it is travelling through time fifty times or a hundred times faster than we are, we can see only one-fiftieth or one-hundredth of it.'

We sat and stared at the empty table for a minute or two. Then the Time Traveller asked us what we thought of it all.

'It sounds believable enough tonight,' said the Medical Man, 'but it will seem different in the morning.'

'Would you like to see the Time Machine itself?' asked the Time Traveller. And then, taking the lamp in his hand, he led the way to the laboratory.

I remember clearly how we all followed him, and how in the laboratory we saw a larger copy of the little machine. It was almost complete, but two bars lay unfinished on the table and I picked one up for a better look.

'Now listen,' said the Medical Man, 'are you really serious?'

'In that machine,' said the Time Traveller, holding the lamp high, 'I intend to travel in time. Is that clear? I was never more serious in my life.'

None of us knew what to say. I looked at Filby over the shoulder of the Medical Man and he smiled at me.

## Chapter 2    The Traveller Returns

I think at that time none of us really believed in the Time Machine. The fact is, the Time Traveller was one of those men who are too clever to be believed. You never felt that you knew everything about him. You always thought that something was hidden, that he was playing a trick on you. If Filby showed us the model and explained things in the Time Traveller's words, we would believe him more easily. We would understand his reasons – because anyone could understand Filby. But the Time Traveller had a strong imagination and we didn't really believe him.

The next Thursday I went to Richmond again and, arriving late, found four or five men already in the sitting room. The Medical Man was standing in front of the fire with a sheet of paper in one hand and his watch in the other. I looked around for the Time Traveller.

'It's half-past seven now,' said the Medical Man. 'I suppose we'd better have dinner?'

'Where's our host?' I asked.

'You have just come? It's rather odd. He has been delayed. He asks me in this note to start dinner at seven if he's not back. He says he will explain when he comes.'

'It seems a pity to let the dinner spoil,' said the editor of a well-known daily paper, and so the Medical Man rang the bell.

Only the Psychologist, the Medical Man and myself had attended the first dinner. The other men were the Editor, a journalist and another – a quiet, shy man with a beard – who I didn't know. There was some discussion at the dinner table about the Time Traveller's absence and I suggested time travelling, in a half-joking way. The Editor wanted that to be explained to him and the Psychologist gave a very dull description of the 'clever trick' we had seen a week before.

He was in the middle of this when the door opened slowly and without noise. I was facing it and saw him first. 'Well!' I said. 'At last!'

The door opened wider and the Time Traveller stood in front of us. I gave a cry of surprise.

'Oh, my friend! What's the matter?' cried the Medical Man, who saw him next.

The others turned towards the door.

He looked very strange. His coat was dusty and dirty, his hair untidy and, it seemed to me, greyer – either with dust or because its colour had gone. His face was very pale and his chin had a cut on it. For a moment he stopped at the door; the light seemed too strong for his eyes. Then he came into the room. He walked slowly, with a bad limp.

He did not say a word, but came painfully to the table and moved a hand towards the wine. The Editor filled a glass and pushed it towards him. He drank it and it seemed to do him good because he looked round the table and smiled a little.

'What have you been doing?' said the Medical Man.

The Time Traveller did not seem to hear. 'Don't let me worry you,' he said in a tired voice. 'I'm all right.' He stopped, held out his glass for more, and drank it down. 'That's good,' he said. His eyes grew brighter, and a faint colour came to his face. Then he spoke again. 'I'm going to wash and dress, and then I'll come down and explain things . . . Save me some of that meat. I'm hungry.' The Editor began a question. 'I'll tell you soon,' said the Time Traveller. 'I'm feeling strange! I'll be all right in a minute.'

He put down his glass and walked towards the door to the stairs. Standing up in my place, I saw his feet as he went out. He had nothing on them except a pair of socks with holes in them. They were covered with dried blood. Then the door closed behind him. For a minute, perhaps, my mind was empty.

'Strange Behaviour of a Famous Scientist,' I heard the Editor say, thinking of his newspaper.

'What's happened to him?' said the Journalist. 'I don't understand.' I thought of the Time Traveller walking painfully upstairs. I don't think anyone else had noticed his limp.

The Medical Man recovered from his surprise first, and rang the bell for a hot plate. The Editor picked up his knife and fork and the Silent Man did the same. The dinner started again. Conversation was slow for a minute or two because we were so surprised. Then the Editor said, 'Does our friend have another job, or just a strong imagination?'

'I feel sure it's this business of the Time Machine,' I said, and continued the Psychologist's story of our earlier meeting. The new guests were very surprised and the Editor said, 'What is this time travelling? A man couldn't cover himself with dust by doing something impossible, could he?'

The Journalist, too, refused to believe it, and started to make a joke of the whole thing. 'Our Special Reporter in the Day after Tomorrow reports,' he was saying – or shouting – when the Time Traveller came back. He was dressed in ordinary evening clothes and nothing except his tired look reminded me of the change that had shocked me.

'Well,' said the Editor, laughing, 'these men say you have been travelling into the middle of next week.'

The Time Traveller sat down without a word. He smiled quietly, in his usual way. 'Where's my meat?' he said. 'How nice it is to stick a fork into meat again.'

'Story!' cried the Editor.

'Later,' said the Time Traveller. 'I want something to eat first. I won't say a word until I get some food into my stomach. Thanks. And the salt.'

'One word,' I said. 'Have you been time travelling?'

'Yes,' said the Time Traveller, with his mouth full.

'I'd give a pound a line for the story in your own words,' said the Editor. The Time Traveller pushed his glass towards the Silent Man, who was staring at his face. He jumped a little, then poured him some wine. The rest of the dinner was uncomfortable. The Journalist tried to relax us by telling funny stories. The Medical Man smoked a cigarette and watched the Time Traveller closely. The Silent Man seemed nervous, and drank a lot of wine.

At last the Time Traveller pushed his plate away and looked round at us. 'I suppose I must apologise,' he said. 'I was so hungry. I've had a most interesting time.' He put out his hand for a cigarette. 'But come into the smoking room. The story is too long to tell over dirty plates.' And he led the way.

'You have told these men about the machine?' he said to me, sitting back in his chair and naming the three new guests.

'But the thing's just a trick,' said the Editor.

'I can't argue tonight. I don't mind telling the story, but I can't argue. I will,' he continued, 'tell you the story of what has happened to me, if you like, but you mustn't interrupt. Most of it will sound like lies, but it is true – every word of it. I was in the laboratory earlier, and since then . . . I have lived eight days . . . days like no human being ever lived before! I am very tired, but I shan't sleep until I have told this thing to you. But no interruptions! Is it agreed?'

We all agreed and the Time Traveller began his story as I have written it down. He sat back in his chair at first and spoke slowly. Afterwards he got more excited. As I write it down I feel the limits of pen and ink, and my own limits. You will read, I expect, with enough attention, but you cannot see the speaker's white, honest face in the bright circle of the little lamp, or hear his voice. Most of us listeners were in shadow. At first each looked at the others. After a time we stopped doing that and looked only at the Time Traveller's face.

## Chapter 3    Forwards in Time

'I told some of you last Thursday how the Time Machine works, and showed you the actual thing itself, incomplete in the laboratory. It is there now, a little damaged by travel, but not in bad condition. I expected to finish it on Friday, but when I had put most of it together, I found that one piece was too short. I had to make this again, and the thing wasn't complete until this morning. So at ten o'clock today, the first of all Time Machines began its journey.

'I checked everything, then got into the seat. I felt a little frightened, but interested in what was going to happen next. I took the starting lever in one hand and the stopping one in the other. Then I pressed the first and almost immediately the second. I felt that I was falling but, looking around, I saw the laboratory exactly as before. Had anything happened? For a moment I thought that my mind had tricked me. Then I noticed the clock. A moment before, it had showed a minute or two past ten. Now it was nearly half-past three.

'I took a breath, held the starting lever with both hands and pushed it harder. The laboratory became unclear and went dark. Mrs Watchett, my cook, came in and walked, without seeing me, towards the garden door. I suppose it took her a minute or two to cross the room, but she seemed to move at high speed. I pressed the lever over to its furthest position.

'The night came, and in another moment came tomorrow. The laboratory grew faint and unclear. Tomorrow night became black, then day again, night again, day again – faster and faster. A low and changing sound filled my ears, and my mind became confused.

'As my speed increased, night followed day faster and faster. The faint picture of the laboratory seemed soon to move away from me. I saw the sun jumping quickly across the sky,

*The laboratory grew faint and unclear.*

once every minute, each minute being a day. I supposed that the laboratory had been destroyed and I had come into the open air. The quick changes of darkness and light were very painful to my eyes. Then, in the short dark times, I saw the moon turning quickly through her quarters from new to full.

'Soon, as I continued, still increasing speed, the change from night to day became one continuous greyness. The sky turned a wonderful deep blue. The jumping sun became a line of fire, the moon a fainter line that changed in width.

'The land was difficult to see clearly. I was still on the hillside where this house now stands. I saw trees growing and changing. They changed from green to brown and back to green again, grew tall, died and fell. I saw enormous buildings rise up, then disappear like dreams. The speed dials on the machine went round faster and faster. The line of the sun moved up and down, from summer to winter, in a minute or less. Minute by minute white snow spread across the world and disappeared, and was followed by the green of spring.

'The unpleasant feelings at the beginning now changed into a kind of crazy excitement. I noticed a strange movement of the machine from side to side, which I couldn't explain, but my mind was too confused to pay any attention to it. So with a kind of madness growing in me, I threw myself into the future. At first I didn't think of stopping. But then a new feeling grew in my mind – a sense of fear mixed with the need to know.

'What strange changes had happened to people? What wonderful improvements to our simple way of life might appear when I looked more closely into that world? I saw large and wonderful buildings growing in front of me, bigger than ours. I saw a stronger green colour move up the hillside, and stay there without any interruption by snow. Although I was travelling so quickly, the world still seemed beautiful, and so my mind turned to stopping the machine.

'My greatest fear was that there would already be something in the space when I, or the machine, stopped. While I travelled at high speed through time, this didn't matter much – I seemed to move like a gas through other things. But when I stopped, I would put myself into whatever lay in my way. Such close contact with the other thing might cause a great explosion. I had thought of this possibility again and again while I was making the machine, but then I had cheerfully accepted it as one of the necessary dangers that a man must face. I wasn't as cheerful now, when I couldn't escape it.

'The strangeness of everything, the movement of the machine and the feeling of continual falling had made me very nervous. I told myself that I could never stop. Then, becoming suddenly angry, I decided to stop immediately. Like a fool in a hurry, I pulled over the lever. The machine turned over and I was thrown through the air.

'There was the sound of thunder in my ears. For a moment I forgot what was happening, then I found myself sitting on soft grass in front of the machine. Heavy rain was falling. Everything still seemed grey, but soon I noticed that the confusion in my ears was gone. I looked around me. I was on a small lawn, surrounded by bushes. Their purple flowers were dropping under the beating of the heavy rain. In a moment I was wet to the skin. "A fine welcome," I thought, "to a man who has travelled so many years to see you."

'Soon I stood up and looked around me. Through the heavy rain I could see an enormous figure cut, perhaps, out of white stone. But the rest of the world was unclear.

'As the rain became lighter, I saw the white figure more clearly. It was very large – a tree touched its shoulder. It was shaped a little like a sphinx with spread wings, and seemed to be flying. The pedestal seemed to be made of metal, and had turned green with age. I stood looking at the figure for some time.

When, at last, I took my eyes from it for a moment, I saw that the rain was stopping and the sky was growing lighter.

'Then I suddenly realised the full danger of my journey. What might appear when the rain stopped? What might people be like? Had they perhaps changed into something inhuman and very strong? I might seem like an old-world wild animal, but more frightening because I looked like them – a horrible creature to be speedily killed.

'Already I saw the shapes of enormous buildings, and a wooded hillside growing clearer through the dying storm. I turned quickly to the Time Machine and tried hard to turn it the right way up. As I did so, the grey rain suddenly stopped and the sun shone through the clouds. My fear grew stronger and I fought hard with the machine. It moved under my attack and turned over. It hit my chin violently. One hand on the seat, the other on the lever, I stood breathing heavily, ready to climb inside it again.

'But now I had a way of escaping, my confidence recovered. I looked with more interest and less fear at this world of the future. In a round opening, high up in the wall of the nearest building, I saw a group of figures wearing soft robes. They had seen me, and their faces were turned towards me.

'Then I heard voices coming nearer. Through the bushes I saw the heads and shoulders of running men. One of these appeared on a path leading straight to the lawn where I stood. He was quite thin, just over a metre high, wearing only a long purple shirt tied at the waist with a leather belt. Noticing that, I realised for the first time how warm the air was.

'He seemed to be very beautiful, but also very weak. At the sight of him, my confidence returned. I took my hands from the machine.

# Chapter 4   The People of the Future

'In another moment we were standing face to face, I and this weak creature from the future. He came straight up to me and laughed into my eyes. I noticed immediately that he had no fear in him. Then he turned to the two others who were following him. He spoke to them in a strange and very sweet-sounding language.

'There were more coming, and soon a little group of perhaps eight or ten of these beautiful people were around me. One of them spoke to me. I don't know why, but I thought that my voice was too strong and deep for them. So I shook my head and, pointing to my ears, shook it again. He came a step forwards, stopped and then touched my hand. Then I felt other soft little hands on my back and shoulders. They wanted to make sure that I was real.

'There was nothing at all frightening in this. In fact, these pretty little people had a relaxed and childlike gentleness that made me confident. And also, they looked so weak that I could imagine myself throwing the whole group of them to the ground.

'But I made a sudden movement to warn them when I saw their little pink hands touching the Time Machine. Fortunately then, when it wasn't too late, I thought of the danger that I had forgotten. Reaching over the bars of the machine, I took out the little levers that would make it move. I put these in my pocket. Then I turned again to the little people to see how I could communicate.

'Looking closer at their faces, I saw some strange differences in their sweet prettiness. They all had the same wavy hair, and this came to a sharp end at the neck and below the ears. There was none growing on their faces, and their ears were very small. Their mouths were small, too, with bright red, rather thin lips. Their little chins came to a point and their eyes were large and gentle. Perhaps my sense of my own importance is too great, but I felt even then that they showed very little interest in me.

'Because they didn't try to speak to me, but simply stood smiling and speaking softly to each other, I began the conversation. I pointed to the Time Machine and to myself. Then, after thinking for a moment how to describe time, I pointed to the sun. At once a pretty little figure dressed in purple and white did the same, and then made the sound of thunder.

'For a moment I was very surprised, though the meaning of his movement was clear enough. The question had come into my mind suddenly: were these people fools? You couldn't really understand how I felt. I had always expected that people living about 800,000 years in the future would have much greater knowledge than us in science, art – everything.

'But one of them had asked me a very simple question, which showed him to be on the level of intelligence of one of our five-year-old children. He had asked me, in fact, if I had come from the sun in a thunderstorm!

'This made me think again about their clothes, their weak arms and legs and pretty faces. A feeling of sadness came into my mind. For a moment I felt that I had built the Time Machine for no reason at all.

'I said yes, pointed to the sun, and made a sound like thunder. This was so real that it frightened them – they all stood back a step or two and bent their heads down. Then one came laughing towards me, carrying some beautiful flowers which were new to me. He put these around my neck.

'The idea made them all happy. Soon they were running around for flowers and throwing them on me until I was almost covered with them. You cannot imagine what wonderful flowers countless years of work had produced.

'Then someone suggested that their new toy should be shown to others in the nearest building, and so I was led past the sphinx made of white stone, which had seemed to watch me all the time with a smile at my surprise. As I went with them, the memory of my hopes for a future full of highly intelligent people came to my mind, and made me smile.

'The building had a very large entrance, and was really enormous. I was worried about the growing crowd of little people, and the shadows beyond the big open doors. Around me I saw many bushes and flowers. It was clear that no gardener was looking after them, but they still looked beautiful. The Time Machine was left on the lawn.

'Several more brightly-dressed people met me in the doorway and we walked through into a large hall. The roof was in shadow and the windows, partly made of coloured glass, let in a soft light. The floor was made of large pieces of a very hard white metal, lower in places where people had clearly walked across it for hundreds of years.

'Along the length of the room were many tables made of shiny stone, perhaps half a metre above the floor, and on these were piles of fruit. Some I recognised as larger apples and oranges, but mostly they were strange.

'The people with me sat down around a table and made signs for me to do the same. They immediately began to eat the fruit with their hands. I was happy to follow their example because I felt thirsty and hungry. As I did so, I took some time to look around the hall and noticed that the glass windows were broken in many places and the curtains were thick with dust. The general effect, though, was very attractive.

'There were, perhaps, a couple of hundred people eating in the hall, and most of them were watching me with interest, their little eyes shining over the fruit they were eating. All of them were wearing the same soft but strong material.

'Fruit, I later learned, was all that they ate. These people of the future didn't eat meat, and while I was with them, although I missed it, I could only eat fruit too. In fact, I discovered later that horses, cows and sheep, and dogs, had disappeared from Earth. But the fruits were very pleasant.

'When I had filled my stomach, I tried to learn some of the language of these new people. The fruits seemed an easy thing to start with, and holding one of these up, I began using questioning sounds and movements. I had great difficulty making them understand. At first they stared in surprise and laughed, but soon a fair-haired little female seemed to realise what I wanted and repeated a name.

'They had to talk for some time to explain things to each other, and when I first tried to make the sounds of their language they were very amused. I felt like a teacher among children, but soon I at least knew a number of names for things and even the verb "to eat".

'It was slow work, though, and the little people soon got tired and wanted to get away from my questions, so I decided to let them give short lessons when they wanted to. And they were very short lessons because I have never met people who are lazier or more easily tired. They used to come to me with happy cries of surprise, like children, but like children they soon stopped examining me and went away to find another toy.

'When the dinner ended, I noted the disappearance of almost all the creatures who had surrounded me at first. It is odd, too, how quickly I stopped caring about these little people. I was continually meeting more of them. They followed me a little distance, talked and laughed around me, smiled in a friendly way, then left me alone.

## Chapter 5   Life in the Future

'The evening was calm as I came out of the great hall, and the land was lit by the colour of the sun as it went down. The big building was on the side of a wide river valley, but the Thames had moved a kilometre or two from its present position. I decided to climb to the top of a hill from where I could see more of our world in the year 802,701. That was the date the little dials of my machine had showed.

'As I walked, I looked for anything that could explain the bad condition of things. A little way up the hill, for example, was a great pile of stones held together by pieces of metal. These were the ruins of a great building, although I couldn't imagine what its use had been.

'Looking round with a sudden thought, I realised that there were no small houses. Here and there among the trees and bushes were palace-like buildings, but the single house, and possibly even the family, had disappeared.

'And then came another thought. I looked at the small group of figures who were following me. I saw that all had the same type of clothes, the same soft hairless faces and the same girlish arms and legs.

'It may seem odd, perhaps, that I hadn't noticed this before. But everything was so strange. Now, I saw the fact clearly enough. These people of the future were all very similar in clothes, and in all other ways the differences between men and women had almost disappeared. And the children seemed to my eyes to be just smaller adults.

'Seeing how safely and comfortably these people lived, I felt that this close similarity of the sexes was understandable. If there are enough people, it becomes a problem rather than an advantage to have a lot of children. If violence comes only rarely and children are safe, there is less need for men to be strong and

19

protect their families. This, I must remind you, was my feeling at the time. Later, I discovered how wrong I was.

'I continued, and because I could walk better than the people of the future, I found myself alone for the first time. At the top of the hill I found a seat of a yellow metal that I didn't recognise. I sat down on it and looked at the wide view of our world under the sunset of that long day. It was as beautiful as I have ever seen. The west was burning gold, mixed with some purple and red. Below was the valley of the Thames, in which the river lay like a line of shining metal.

'As I watched, I began to try to understand the things I had seen. (Afterwards I realised I had only learned half the truth.) It seemed to me that people were now past their best. The sunset made me think about the sunset of our people. For the first time I began to understand an odd result of the social changes we are trying to make at the moment. Strength comes because we need to be strong; weakness comes when we feel safe. The work of improving the conditions of life, of making life safer and safer, had continued until nothing more could be done. The result was what I saw!

'The science of our time has attacked only a few human diseases, but it moves forwards. Farming today is still at an early stage. We improve our plants and animals very slowly – a new and better apple, a prettier and larger flower, a cow that gives more milk. One day the whole world will be better organised, and better.

'I knew that this change had been made, and made well, in the space of time across which my machine had jumped. The air was free of unpleasant insects, the earth was free of useless plants. Everywhere there were fruits and sweet and pleasant flowers. Beautiful birds flew here and there. And I saw no diseases during my stay.

'Social changes, too, had been made. I saw people living in fine buildings, beautifully dressed, but I hadn't yet found them doing any work. There were no signs of economic activity. The shop, the advertisement, buying and selling – all of these things are so important to us, and all of them were gone. It was natural in the evening that I had the idea of a social heaven.

'But this change in conditions has to produce changes in people. What is the cause of human intelligence and energy? Difficulties make people strong and clever and help them to work together. And the family, with its protective love and selfishness, is there for the care of children. The love of parents helps to keep the young out of danger. *Now*, where were these dangers?

'I thought of the physical smallness of the people, their low intelligence and those big ruined buildings. It strengthened my belief that humans, who had always fought against nature, had finally won – because after the fight comes quietness. People had been strong, energetic and intelligent, and had used this energy to change their living conditions. And now they too had changed because of the new conditions.

'No doubt the beauty of the buildings was the result of the last waves of the now purposeless energy of people. After that, they began to lead quieter lives. Even artistic activity would finally disappear – had almost disappeared in the time I saw. The people liked to cover themselves in flowers, to dance and to sing in the sunlight. That was all they did.

'As I stood there in the growing dark, I thought that I had understood the whole secret of these pleasant people. Possibly their population control had worked too well, and their numbers had fallen instead of staying the same. That would explain the empty ruins. My explanation was very simple, and believable enough – as most wrong ideas are!

# Chapter 6   Lost in Time

'As I stood there thinking about this too perfect success of humans, the full moon came up in the north-east. The little figures stopped moving around below me and the night began to feel cold. I decided to go down and find a place to sleep.

'I looked for the building I knew. Then my eye moved to the white sphinx on the pedestal. There were the bushes and there was the little lawn. I looked at it again. A strange doubt made me feel cold. "No," I said to myself, "that isn't the lawn."

'But it *was* the lawn, because the white face of the sphinx was towards it. Can you imagine how I felt as I realised this? But you can't. The Time Machine had gone!

'At once I understood the possibility of losing my own time, of being left helpless in this strange new world. I ran with great jumps down the hillside. Once I fell and cut my face. I did nothing to stop the blood, but jumped up and continued running. All the time I was saying to myself, "They have just pushed it under the bushes out of the way."

'But I knew that I was wrong. I suppose I covered the whole distance to the small lawn, three kilometres perhaps, in ten minutes. I shouted but nobody answered. Nobody seemed to be moving in that moonlit world.

'When I reached the lawn, I found that my worst fears were true. The Time Machine was nowhere to be seen. I felt faint and cold. I ran round the lawn quickly, checking every corner, then stopped suddenly. Above me was the white sphinx. It seemed to smile with pleasure at my problems.

'It is possible that the little people had put the machine in a safe place for me, but I didn't feel that they were either strong enough or caring enough to move it. This is what worried me, the feeling of a new power that had moved the machine. But where could it be?

22

*The Time Machine was nowhere to be seen.*

'I think I went a little mad. I remember running violently in and out of the moonlit bushes all round the sphinx and frightening a small white animal that I didn't recognise. Then, crying and shouting, I went down to the great building of stone. The big hall was dark, silent and empty. I lit a match and continued past the dusty curtains.

'There I found a second great hall, where about twenty of the little people were sleeping. I have no doubt they found my second appearance strange, as I came suddenly out of the quiet darkness with mad noises and the sudden light of a match. Perhaps they had forgotten about matches. "Where is my Time Machine?" I began, shaking them with my hands.

'This behaviour was very strange to them. Some laughed, but most looked very frightened. When I saw them standing round me, I realised that it was foolish to try and frighten them. Judging by their daylight behaviour, I thought that fear must be forgotten.

'I threw down the match and, knocking one of the people over as I went, I ran across the big dining-hall again, out under the moonlight. I heard cries of terror and their little feet running this way and that. I don't remember everything I did as the moon moved slowly up the sky. I know that I ran here and there screaming, then lay on the ground near the sphinx and cried. After that I slept, and when I woke up again it was light.

'I sat up in the freshness of the morning, trying to remember how I had got there. Then things became clear in my mind. I understood the wild stupidity of my madness overnight and I could reason with myself. "Suppose the worst," I said. "Suppose the machine is really lost – perhaps destroyed? I should be calm and patient, learn the ways of the people, learn what has happened and how to get materials and tools – then, in the end, perhaps, I can make another machine." That would be my only hope, perhaps, but better than giving up. And it was a beautiful and interesting world.

'But probably the machine had only been taken away. I must be calm, find its hiding-place and get it back by force and cleverness. I stood up and looked around me, wondering where I could wash. I felt tired and dirty and rather surprised by my emotional state the night before.

'I made a careful examination of the ground around the little lawn. I wasted some time in useless questions, asked, as well as I could, to the little people that passed. They all failed to understand what I meant. Some simply said nothing; others thought it was a joke and laughed at me.

'The grass told me more. I found a line in it. There were other signs around, with strange narrow footprints. This made me look again at the pedestal. It was made, as I think I have said, of metal. It was highly decorated with metal panels on either side.

'I went and knocked at these. The pedestal was hollow. There was no way to pull to open the panels, but perhaps if they were doors they opened from inside. One thing was clear enough to my mind: it wasn't difficult to work out that the Time Machine was inside that pedestal. But how had it got there?

'I saw the heads of two people dressed in orange coming through the bushes towards me. They came and, pointing to the pedestal, I tried to make them understand my wish to open it. But at my first move to do this they behaved very oddly. I don't know how to describe their faces to you. They looked insulted.

'I tried a sweet-looking man in white next, with exactly the same result. He made me feel ashamed of myself. But as you know, I wanted the Time Machine and I tried him again. As he turned away, like the others, I lost my temper. In three steps I was after him, took him by the loose part of his robe round the neck and began pulling him towards the pedestal. Then I saw the fear on his face and I let him go.

'But I wasn't beaten yet. I hit the metal panels with my hands. I thought I heard something move inside – to be exact, I thought

I heard a sound like a laugh – but perhaps I was mistaken. Then I got a big stone from the river and hit the metal until I had flattened part of the decoration. The little people could hear the noise a kilometre way in all directions, but they did nothing.

'I saw a crowd of them on the hillside, looking at me in a frightened way. At last, hot and tired, I sat down to watch the place. But I was too impatient to watch for long. I could work at a problem for years, but I was unable to wait, inactive, for twenty-four hours.

'I got up after a time and began walking aimlessly through the bushes towards the hill again. "Patience," I said to myself. "If you want your machine again, you must leave that pedestal alone. If they intend to take your machine away, it won't help if you destroy their metal panels. If they don't, you will get it back when you can ask for it.

' "Face this world. Learn its ways, watch it, be careful of guessing its meaning too quickly. In the end you will find an answer to it all." Then suddenly the humour of the situation came into my mind: the thought of the years I had spent in study and work to get into the future age, and now my impatience to get out of it. I had put myself into the most hopeless situation a man could ever imagine. I couldn't help laughing at myself.


## Chapter 7   Ghosts

'Going through the big palace, it seemed to me that the little people were staying away from me. Perhaps it was my imagination, or because I had hit the metal panels. I was careful, though, to show no worry and not try to catch any of them, and after a day or two the situation got back to normal.

'I decided to put any thought of my Time Machine and the

mystery of the metal doors as much as possible in a corner of my memory. I hoped that in the end, growing knowledge would lead me back to them in a natural way. But you can understand why I stayed within a circle of a few kilometres around my point of arrival.

'As far as I could see, all the world seemed to be like the Thames valley. From every hill I saw the same large numbers of fine buildings, all very different in material and style, and the same kinds of trees and bushes. I soon noticed, though, a number of wells in the ground. Several of these, it seemed to me, were very deep. One lay by a path up the hill, which I had followed during my first walk. Like the others, it had a top made of metal, interestingly decorated and protected by a little roof from the rain.

'Sitting by the side of these wells, and looking down into the darkness, I could see no sign of water or any reflection when I lit a match. But in all of them I heard a certain sound like the beating of a big engine. I also discovered, from the flames of my matches, that air was going down into them. I threw a piece of paper down into one and, instead of falling slowly, it was at once pulled quickly out of sight. I couldn't imagine what these wells were for.

'And I must say now that I learned very little about many parts of the life of these people. Let me describe my difficulties. I went into several big palaces, but they were just living places, great dining-halls and sleeping apartments. I could find no machines of any kind, but these people were dressed in fine cloth that didn't seem very old, and their shoes, though undecorated, were very well made.

'But the people didn't seem to make things themselves. There were no shops, no factories, no signs that they brought things in from other places. They spent all their time playing gently, swimming in the river, falling in love in a half-playful way, eating fruit and sleeping. I couldn't see how or where things were produced.

'But something had taken the Time Machine into the pedestal. Why? I couldn't imagine. Suppose you found something written in English, with here and there some words that were completely unknown to you. Well, on the third day of my visit, that was how I felt about the world of 802,701.

'That day I made a friend – a kind of friend. As I was watching some of the little people playing in a shallow part of the river, one of them was suddenly pulled away by the water. The river there could run quite quickly, but not too quickly for a swimmer of normal ability. It will give you an idea, therefore, of the weakness of these people, when I tell you that none tried to help the one that was in such danger.

'When I realised this, I quickly took off my clothes and, walking into the water at a place lower down, I caught her and brought her safely to land.

'She soon began to feel better and I saw that she was all right before I left her. I had such a low opinion of her people by then that I didn't expect any thanks from her. I was wrong about that, though.

'This happened in the morning. In the afternoon I met my little woman as I was returning from a long walk, and she greeted me with cries of happiness and gave me some flowers. Perhaps because I had been very lonely I did my best to show I was happy with the gift. We were soon sitting together and deep in a conversation, mainly of smiles.

'The woman's friendliness affected me exactly as a child's would. We passed each other flowers and she kissed my hands. I did the same to hers. Then I tried to talk, and found that her name was Weena. That was the beginning of a strange friendship, which continued for a week and ended . . . as I will tell you!

'She was exactly like a child. She wanted to be with me

always. She wanted to follow me everywhere, and on my next journey around the area I walked fast and tried to leave her behind. She gave up at last, calling after me rather sadly. But the problems of the world had to be solved and I hadn't, I said to myself, come into the future to start a relationship.

'She was, though, a very great comfort. When it was too late, only when it was too late, I clearly understood how badly she felt when I left her, and what she meant to me. By seeming fond of me, and by showing in her weak way that she cared for me, the little person soon gave my returns to the place of the white sphinx almost the feeling of coming home. I used to watch for her when I came over the hill.

'From her, too, I learned that fear had not yet left the world. She was fearless enough in the daylight, but she hated the dark shadows. Darkness to her was the one thing to be frightened of. It was a very strong emotion, and I started thinking and watching.

'I discovered then, among other things, that these people got together in the great houses after dark and slept in groups. I never found one outside, alone. And if I entered the room without a light, I made them very afraid. But I was such a fool that I missed the lesson of that fear, and although it made Weena unhappy I slept away from the others.

'It worried her greatly, but in the end her feelings for me won. For five of the nights of our friendship, including the last night of all, she slept with her head on my arm. But my story is running away from me as I speak of her.

'On the night before I met her I was woken very early in the morning. I had slept badly, dreaming that I was under water, and that fish were touching my face. I woke suddenly and with the odd feeling that a greyish animal had just rushed out of the room.

'I tried to go to sleep again, but I felt uncomfortable. It was that grey hour when things are just appearing from the darkness, but are still unreal. I got up, went down into the great hall and out onto the stones in front of the palace. I thought I would go and watch the sun come up.

'The moon was going down, and the dying moonlight and the first light of day were mixed in a pale half-light. The bushes were inky black, the ground a dark grey, and up on the hillside I thought I could see ghosts. Three times I saw white figures and twice I thought I saw a single white animal running quickly on two legs.

'Near the ruins I saw a group of them carrying a dark body. They moved quickly and it seemed that they disappeared among the bushes. The light was still unclear, you must understand. I was experiencing that cold, uncertain, early-morning feeling you may know, and I doubted my eyes.

'As the eastern sky grew brighter, and the light of day brought stronger colours to the world again, I watched the hillside closely. But I saw no more white figures. I thought about them all morning – or at least until I had to get Weena out of the river. I connected them in some way with the white animal I had touched in my first mad search for the Time Machine. It was more pleasant to think about Weena, but these ghosts would soon take much stronger control of my mind.

## Chapter 8   Morlocks

'I think I said how much hotter the weather of this Golden Age was than our own. I can't explain this. It is usual to think that the sun will continue cooling in the future. But people forget that the Earth must also, in the end, fall back closer and closer to the sun.

'Well, one very hot morning – my fourth, I think – as I was

trying to get away from the heat and the strong light in a large ruin near the great house, a strange thing happened. Climbing among those piles of stones, I found a narrow room, whose end and side windows were closed by falling stones. After the light outside, it seemed very dark to me. I entered it, feeling my way with my hands.

'Suddenly, I stopped and held my breath. A pair of eyes, made bright by the reflection of the daylight outside, was watching me out of the darkness.

'I felt the old natural fear of wild animals as I looked into those angry eyes. I was afraid to turn. Then I thought how safely people appeared to be living. And then I remembered their strange terror of the dark.

'Trying to control my fear, I took a step forwards and spoke. My voice was strong but shaking. I put out my hand and touched something soft.

'At once the eyes moved to the side and something white ran past me. I turned, as my heart beat even faster, and saw an odd-looking figure, its head held down in a strange way, running across the sunlit space behind me. It ran into a large stone, fell to one side and in a moment was hidden in a black shadow under another pile of stones.

'It went too fast for me to see clearly, but I know it was a dull white and had strange large greyish-red eyes. Also, there was fair hair on its head and down its back. I can't say whether it ran on four legs or only with its arms held very low. After a few seconds I followed it into the second pile of ruins.

'I couldn't find it at first, but after some time in the deep darkness I saw one of those round well-like openings that I have told you about, half-closed by a large fallen stone. A sudden thought came to me. Had the thing disappeared down the well?

'I lit a match and, looking down, saw a small white moving

*It stared at me as it climbed down.*

creature with large bright eyes. It stared at me as it climbed down. Now I saw for the first time a kind of metal ladder down the side of the well. Then the light burned my fingers and fell out of my hand, going out as it dropped. I lit another but the horrible little creature had disappeared.

'I don't know how long I sat staring down that well. Time passed before I could make myself believe that I had seen something human. But slowly I began to understand the truth: that humans hadn't stayed as one species, but had become two different animals. My pleasant children of the Upper-world weren't alone.

'And what, I wondered, was this creature of the dark doing in my idea of a perfectly organised society? What was its relationship with the calm laziness of the beautiful Upper-world people? And what was hidden down there? I sat on the edge of the well telling myself that there was nothing to fear and that I must go down to find the answer. But I was very afraid to go! As I sat there, two of the Upper-world people came running across the daylight into the shadow. The male followed the female, throwing flowers at her as he ran.

'They seemed upset to find me looking down the well. I understood that it was bad behaviour to look down these holes, because when I pointed to this one and tried to make a question about it in their language, they grew even more upset and turned away. But they were interested in my matches and I struck some to amuse them. I asked them again about the well, and again I failed. So I soon left them, intending to go back to Weena and see what she could tell me.

'But my mind was already working. I now had an idea of the importance of these wells, of the mystery of the ghosts, of the meaning of the metal panels and what had happened to the Time Machine! And I also had the beginnings of a solution to the economic mystery that had worried me.

'Here was my new idea. Clearly, this second human species lived underground. There were three things especially which made me think this. First, there was the white skin common to most animals that live largely in the dark. Then there were those large eyes, like those of a cat. Finally, its confusion in the sunshine, how it ran into the stones, the strange way it held its head – all these things made me believe that its eyes weren't used to the light.

'Under my feet, then, there must be many tunnels, where these people lived. The wells, which carried air to them, were all along the hillsides – everywhere, in fact, except along the river valley. Their great number showed how many tunnels there were. It seemed natural, too, to believe that the underground people made things for the comfort of the daylight people. The idea was so sensible that I accepted it at once, and then thought about how humans had turned into two species.

'Starting with the problems of our own age, it seemed clear to me that the widening of the social difference between the worker and the manager explained the whole situation. Even now we can see the beginnings of this. We have begun to make use of underground space – we have railways, underground workrooms and restaurants, and these are becoming more common.

'It was clear, I thought, that workers had begun to go underground into larger and larger factories, spending more and more of their time there, until, in the end –!

'Also, the increasing difference between the social classes made marriage between them less and less frequent. So above the ground now were the Haves, looking for pleasure and comfort and beauty, and below ground the Have-nots, the workers, changed by the demands of their jobs.

'When they were there, they had to pay rent, and not a little of it, for the air coming to their homes. If they refused, they would die. If they couldn't live in this way, they would also die. In the end, everyone living underground would be used to the conditions of their life, and as happy in their way as the Upper-world people were.

'This, I must warn you, was my explanation at the time. It may be completely wrong but I still think it is the best one. But I think this way of life had worked better in the past. The Upper-world people had become too safe, and so had become smaller, weaker and less intelligent.

'I didn't yet know what had happened to the underground people. But I could imagine that the changes to the Morlocks – that, I discovered later, was their name – were even greater than the changes to the Eloi, the ones I already knew.

'Then came worrying doubts. Why had the Morlocks taken my Time Machine? I felt sure they had taken it. Why, too, if the Eloi were in control, could they not get my machine back for me? And why were they so terribly afraid of the dark? As I have said, I questioned Weena about this Under-world, but I learned nothing from her.

'At first she didn't understand my questions and later she refused to answer them. The whole subject seemed too unpleasant. And when I asked her again, perhaps a little loudly, she began to cry. They were the only tears, except my own, that I ever saw in that Golden Age.

'When I saw those tears, I stopped worrying about the Morlocks. I lit a match and very soon she was smiling again.

## Chapter 9   Underground

'It may seem odd to you, but it was two days before I could find out more about the Morlocks. I felt a strange fear of those pale bodies. They were just the same colour as the things one sees in jars in a museum and they were horribly cold when you touched them. I knew I could only get to the Time Machine by going underground. But I couldn't do it. I was so alone, and even the idea of climbing down into the darkness of the well frightened me.

'The next night I did not sleep well. Probably my health had suffered a little. I was confused and unhappy. Once or twice I had a feeling of great fear for which I could see no definite reason. I remember walking noiselessly into the great hall where the little people were sleeping – that night Weena was among them – and feeling more comfortable in their company. I realised that the moon was in its last quarter and the nights were growing darker, and that there might be more appearances of those unpleasant creatures from below. And on both these days I had the restless feeling of someone who is trying to escape a duty. I felt that I could only get the Time Machine back if I understood these underground mysteries. But I wasn't brave enough to solve the mysteries, and I never quite felt safe.

'These worries drove me further and further in my walks around the country. Going south-west towards the higher country, I saw, far away, an enormous building. It was larger than the largest of the palaces or ruins I knew, and the front was pale green. The difference in appearance suggested a difference in use, and I thought about going to look around. But it was growing late so I decided to wait until the following day, and I returned to Weena's welcome.

'But the next morning I realised that my interest in the Green Palace was just helping me to delay an experience I was afraid of. I decided that I would go down without wasting any more time, and walked in the early morning towards a well near the ruins.

'Little Weena danced beside me to the well, but when she saw me bend over the opening and look down, she seemed upset. "Goodbye, little Weena," I said, kissing her, and then I began to feel over the edge for the metal steps.

'At first she watched me with surprise. Then she gave a most heartbreaking cry and, running to me, began to pull at me with her little hands. I think her fear made me braver. I shook her off and in another moment I was inside the well. I saw her frightened face over the top and smiled to make her feel better.

'I had to climb down a well perhaps two hundred metres deep. There were metal bars all the way down, but these were made for a person much smaller and lighter than I was and I was quickly tired by the climb. And not simply tired! One of the bars bent suddenly under my weight and almost threw me off into the blackness below. For the moment I hung by one hand, and after that I didn't dare to rest again.

'Although my arms and back were very painful, I continued climbing down as quickly as possible. Looking up, I saw the opening, a small blue circle, where Weena's head was round and black. The noise of a machine grew louder. Everything except that little circle above was very dark, and when I looked up again she had disappeared.

'I was in great discomfort and thought of going up again. But I continued to climb down. At last, with great happiness, I saw, half a metre to the right of me, a thin opening in the wall. Pulling myself in, I found it was the start of a narrow tunnel in which I could lie down and rest. It was not too soon.

'I lay there, I don't know how long, until I felt a soft hand touching my face. Quickly getting to my feet in the darkness, I pulled out my matches. I struck one and saw three white figures moving quickly back, away from the light. Their eyes, unusually large from living in darkness, were like those of deep-water fish, and reflected the light in the same way. I have no doubt they could see me and they didn't seem to have any fear of me, only of the light.

'The thought of running away was still in my mind, but I told myself that the job had to be done. As I felt my way along the tunnel, the noise of machinery grew louder. Soon I came to a large open space and, striking another match, saw that I had entered an enormous underground room. It stretched into total darkness beyond my light.

'Great shapes like large machines rose out of the darkness, and made strange shadows in which I could see the shapes of Morlocks hiding. The air wasn't very fresh and there was a faint smell of fresh blood. Some way down the central path was a little table of white metal, covered with food. So the Morlocks, at least, were meat-eaters!

'Even at the time, I remember wondering what large animal still lived to produce the red piece of meat that I saw. Then the match burned down to my fingers and fell, a moving red spot in the darkness.

'I have thought since then how very badly-prepared I was for such an experience. When I had started building the Time Machine, I had had the stupid idea that the people of the future would certainly be far ahead of us in all their inventions. I had come without weapons, without medicine, without tobacco, even without enough matches.

'I didn't even think of bringing a camera, so I couldn't take a picture of that Under-world, to examine later. I stood there with only the weapons that nature had given me – hands, feet and teeth – and the four matches that I had left.

I was afraid to push my way in among all this machinery in the dark, and then I discovered that I had almost finished my matches. I had never thought that there was any need to save them and I had wasted almost half the box surprising the Eloi. Now I had four left, and while I stood in the dark a hand touched mine and cold fingers began feeling my face.

'I thought I could hear the breathing of a crowd of those horrible little creatures around me. I felt the box of matches in my hand being gently pulled away, and other hands behind me pulling at my clothes. I shouted as loudly as I could.

'They jumped back, and then I could feel them coming towards me again. They took hold of me more strongly, whispering odd sounds to each other. I shook violently and shouted again. This time they weren't so worried, and they made a strange laughing noise as they came back at me.

'I was horribly frightened. I decided to strike another match and escape under the protection of its light. I did so and, keeping the flame burning with a piece of paper from my pocket, I moved quickly into the narrow tunnel. But I had just entered this when my light was blown out, and in the blackness I could hear the Morlocks hurrying after me.

'In a moment I was held by several hands, trying to pull me back. I struck another light and waved it in their faces. You can't imagine how horribly inhuman they looked in their blindness and surprise. But I didn't stay. I moved back again and when my second match went out, I struck my third. It had almost burned down when I reached the opening into the well.

'I lay down on the edge and felt for the metal bars. As I did so, my feet were held from behind and I was violently pulled backwards. I lit my last match . . . and it went out. But I had my hand on the bars now and, kicking violently, I got myself free of the hands of the Morlocks and quickly climbed up the well. They stayed, afraid of the light, all except one little one who followed me for some way, and almost got my shoe as a prize.

'That climb never seemed to end. In the last eight or ten metres of it, a terrible feeling of sickness came over me. I had the greatest difficulty holding the bars. Several times I thought that I might fall. At last, though, I got over the top of the well, and walked shakily out of the ruin into the blinding sunlight.

'I fell on my face. Even the earth felt sweet and clean. Then I remember Weena kissing my hands and ears, and the voices of others among the Eloi. Then, for a time, I remember nothing.

# Chapter 10    A Place to Live

'Now I seemed in a worse position than before. Until then, except during my night of madness over the disappearance of the Time Machine, I had felt that in the end I would escape. But that hope was shaken by these new discoveries. I had been worried by the thought of unknown forces which I could beat when I understood them. The situation was different now. There was something sickening about the Morlocks – something inhuman. Before, I had felt like a man who had fallen into a hole: my worry was how to get out of it. Now I felt like an animal which had been caught, whose enemy would come to him soon.

'That enemy was the darkness of the new moon. Weena had put this fear into my head by some things she said, which at first I didn't understand, about the Dark Nights. Now I could guess what the coming Dark Nights might mean. The moon was getting smaller and each night there was a longer time of darkness. And I now understood a little of the Eloi's fear of the dark. I wondered what terrible things the Morlocks did under the new moon.

'The Eloi had probably been the managers and the Morlocks their servants, but that situation had changed a long time before. The two species were moving towards, or had already arrived at, a completely new relationship. The Eloi were still allowed to own the world, because the Morlocks, underground for so long, now found the daylight impossible. And the Morlocks made their clothes, I thought, and did other necessary things for them, perhaps because an old habit of service had continued.

'But clearly, the end of the Eloi's power was coming closer. And suddenly I thought of the meat I had seen in the Under-world. I tried to remember its shape. I had a feeling it was something familiar, but I hadn't recognised it at the time.

40

'The little people could do nothing about their fear, but I was made differently. I came out of our age, this best time for humans, when fear doesn't make us helpless. I at least could defend myself. Without further delay I decided to make myself weapons and a safe place where I could sleep. From there, I could face this strange world with some of that confidence. I had been slow to realise what creatures could harm me night after night. I felt I could never sleep again until my bed was safe from them. I shook with fear to think how they had already examined me.

'I walked during the afternoon along the valley of the Thames, but found nowhere that seemed safe. All the buildings and trees seemed easy for such good climbers as the Morlocks to get into, judging by their skill at entering and leaving their wells. Then the Green Palace came into my mind. In the evening, carrying Weena like a child on my shoulders, I went up into the hills towards the south-west. The distance, I had thought, was eleven or twelve kilometres, but it was probably nearer thirty.

'I had first seen the place on a wet afternoon when things in the distance seemed nearer. In addition, the heel of one of my shoes was loose, so I couldn't walk well. And it was already long past sunset when I came in sight of the palace, dark against the pale yellow of the sky.

'Weena had been very pleased when I began to carry her, but later she wanted me to put her down. She ran along by my side, occasionally going off to pick flowers to put in my pockets. Weena had been unsure of the purpose of pockets, but had decided that they should be filled and decorated with flowers. And that reminds me! While changing my jacket I found . . .'

The Time Traveller paused, put his hand into his pocket and silently placed two dead flowers on the little table. Then he went back to his story.

'As the quiet of evening spread over the world and we moved

over the top of the hill towards Wimbledon, Weena grew tired and wanted to return to the house of grey stone. But I pointed to the Green Palace, and tried to make her understand that we were looking for a safe place there.

'You know that quietness that comes before dark? In that calm my senses seemed to sharpen. I thought that I could almost see the tunnels in the ground under my feet – that I could see the Morlocks going here and there and waiting for the dark. In my excitement I imagined that they would see my arrival in their homes as an act of war.

'So we continued and the evening turned into night. The ground grew difficult to see and the trees turned black. Weena's fears and her tiredness grew. I took her in my arms and talked to her. Then, as the darkness grew deeper, she put her arms round my neck. Closing her eyes, she tightly pressed her face against my shoulder.

'So we went down a long hillside into a valley, and there in the poor light I almost fell into a little river. I walked across this and went up the opposite side. I had seen nothing of the Morlocks, but it was still early in the night. The darker hours before the moon came up hadn't yet arrived.

'From the top of the next hill I saw a thick wood spreading wide and black in front of me. I stopped at this. I could see no end to it, either to the right or the left. Feeling tired – my feet, especially, were very painful – I carefully lowered Weena from my shoulder as I stopped, and sat down on the grass. I could no longer see the Green Palace, and I wasn't sure of my direction.

'I looked into the thickness of the wood and thought of what it might hide. In there, we might be out of sight of the stars. Even if there were no other waiting danger, there would still be many things to fall over and walk into. I was very tired, too, after the excitement of the day, so I decided that I wouldn't face it, but would spend the night on the open hill.

*I pointed to the Green Palace.*

'Weena, I was glad to find, was asleep. I put my jacket round her and sat down beside her to wait for the moon to rise. The hillside was quiet and empty, but from the black of the wood came, now and then, the sound of living things. Above me the stars shone, because the night was very clear, and I felt a sense of friendly comfort from their lights. All the familiar old ones had moved in the sky, rearranged in new groups during countless human lifetimes.

'As I looked at all these stars, I suddenly felt that my problems were smaller. I thought of their distance, and their slow movements out of the unknown past into the unknown future. And in my time travelling forwards, all the activity, the traditions, the organisations, the nations, languages, literature, hopes, even the memory of humans as I knew them, had totally disappeared. Instead, there were these weak people who had forgotten their great history, and the white Things of which I was so afraid.

'Then I thought of the great fear between the two species. I thought about the meat that I had seen. And for the first time I understood what it might be. But the thought was too horrible! I looked at little Weena sleeping beside me, her face white under the stars, and put the thought from my mind.

'Through that long night I kept my mind off the Morlocks as well as I could. I passed the time by trying to find signs of the old groups of stars in the sky. No doubt I slept a little. Then, as time passed, there came a soft light in the eastern sky and the old moon came up, thin and pointed and white. And close behind, and stronger, came the light from the sun.

'No Morlocks had come near us. In fact, I had seen none on the hills that night. And in the confidence of the new day it almost seemed to me that I had been wrong to be afraid. I stood up and found my foot with the loose heel was painful, so I sat down again, took off my shoes and threw them away.

'I woke Weena and we went down into the wood, now green

44

and pleasant instead of black and unwelcoming. We found some fruit there to eat for breakfast. We soon met other Eloi, laughing and dancing in the sunlight. And then I thought again of the meat that I had seen. I felt sure now what it was and with all my heart I pitied them.

'Clearly, at some time in the past, the Morlocks hadn't been able to find enough food. Possibly they had lived on rats and similar animals. Now the Eloi were like fat cows, which the Morlocks kept and hunted. And there was Weena dancing at my side!

'I tried to think more scientifically, and less emotionally. Perhaps this was a punishment for human selfishness. Some people had been happy to live from the work of others. They had said this was necessary, and in time it had become equally necessary for the workers to eat them. But this attitude was impossible. It didn't matter how unintelligent they were, the Eloi still looked human. I understood their situation and I felt their fear.

'I had at that time no clear ideas about what I should do. I thought I could find a safe place and make myself some weapons out of metal or stone. Next I hoped to find a way of making fire, so I would have the weapon of a torch. I knew that nothing would work better against these Morlocks. Then I wanted to find a way of breaking open the metal panels under the white sphinx.

'I felt that if I could enter those doors and carry a light in front of me I would discover the Time Machine and escape. I couldn't imagine that the Morlocks were strong enough to move it far away. I had decided to bring Weena with me to our own time. And thinking about plans like these, we walked towards the building which I had chosen as our home.

## Chapter 11   The Green Palace

I found the Green Palace, when we came to it at about midday, to be empty and falling into ruin. The glass in its windows was broken and large pieces of green material had fallen off the walls onto the ground. It stood high on a grassy hill and, looking towards the north-east before I entered it, I was surprised to see a large river where I thought Wandsworth and Battersea had been in the past. I thought then of what had happened or might be happening to the living things in the sea.

'Along the front of the palace I saw writing in an unknown language. I thought, rather foolishly, that Weena might help to understand this, but I only learned that the idea of writing had never entered her head. She always seemed to me, I imagine, more human than she was, perhaps because her love was so human.

Inside the large door – which was open and broken – we found, instead of the usual hall, a long room lit by many side windows. At first look I was reminded of a museum. The floor was thick with dust, and an interesting collection of strange objects was covered in grey dust too. Then I noticed, in the centre of the room, the bones of a large animal. They lay on the floor in the thick dust, and in one place, where the rainwater had come through the roof, some had almost been destroyed.

'This made me feel sure that I was in a museum. Going towards the side I found shelves and on them I found the old familiar glass cases of our time. They had kept the air out; the objects inside were still in good condition.

'I continued walking and found another short room running across the end of the first. This appeared to be full of rocks, in which I had little interest, so we didn't stop. The next room appeared to be about natural history, but everything had changed so much that it was unrecognisable. A few blackened things which had been animals many years before, a brown dust of dead plants, that was all! I was sorry about that, because I wanted to know how people had learned to control nature.

'Then we came to an enormous room, which was very badly-lit. Every few metres, white glass balls hung from the ceiling – many of them broken – which suggested that the place had had electric lighting. On either side of me were large machines, all in bad condition and many broken down, but some still quite complete. I wanted to stay among these because I could only make guesses at what they were for. I thought that if I could learn to understand them, I would have powers that might be useful against the Morlocks.

'Suddenly Weena came very close to my side, so suddenly that she surprised me. I woke out of my dream and then noticed that the floor of the room went downhill. I had come in at an end that was above ground, and had a few tall thin windows. As you went down the room, the ground came up against these windows, until finally there was only a narrow line of daylight at the top.

'I had moved slowly, thinking about the machines, and had been too interested in them to notice that it was getting dark. Then Weena's increasing nervousness made me realise that the room ran down into thick darkness. I stopped and, as I looked around me, I saw that the dust was thinner there. Further away towards the darkness, it appeared to be broken by a number of small, narrow footprints.

'I felt that I was wasting my time looking at this machinery. I remembered that it was already late in the afternoon and that I still had no weapon, no safe place and no way of making a fire. And then down at the far end of the room I heard the sound of footsteps and the same strange noises I had heard down the well.

'I took Weena's hand. Then, getting a sudden idea, I left her and turned to a machine on which there was a long metal bar. Climbing up, and taking this in my hands, I put all my weight on

47

it sideways. It broke after a few seconds, and I rejoined Weena with a weapon in my hand. It was heavy enough, I thought, to break the head of any Morlock I might meet. And I wanted very much to kill a Morlock or two. I wanted to go straight down the room and kill the ones I heard. I didn't do this, though, partly because I also wanted to stay with Weena – and to get back to my Time Machine.

'Well, with the metal bar in one hand and Weena in the other, I went out of that room and into another even larger one, which was full of old books. These had fallen to pieces and none of the words could be read. I'm not a great writer, so didn't spend too long thinking about this waste of time and energy, but I did think sadly of my own seventeen papers on scientific subjects.

'Then, going up the wide stairs, we came to a room that had perhaps been a science room. And here I had some hopes of finding something useful. Except at one end where the roof had fallen down, this room was in good condition. I went quickly to every unbroken case. At last, in one of them, I found a box of matches. Very excited, I tried them. They were dry and perfectly good.

'I turned to Weena. "Dance," I said to her in her own language, because now I really had a weapon against the horrible creatures that we were afraid of. And so, in that broken-down museum, on the thick, soft carpet of dust, to Weena's great happiness, I danced a slow dance, singing a song as well as I could. Partly the dance was from different countries, partly it was my own invention – because I am naturally inventive, as you know.

'It was strange that this box of matches had lasted for so many years, but it was very fortunate for me. And I also found something even less likely – a jar containing a number of candles. I broke it open, put these in my pocket and left that room very happy.

'I can't tell you all the story of that long afternoon. I would have to think hard to remember what I saw in the correct order. I remember a long room filled with guns, and although some were still in good condition, I could find no bullets. In another place was a large collection of stone and metal gods – Polynesian, Mexican, Greek, Roman, from every country on Earth, I think. And here I couldn't help writing my name on the nose of a stone god from South America that I really liked.

'As evening came, my interest level fell. I went through room after room: dusty, silent, often ruined. Some things were just piles of broken material; some were in better condition. In the end we came to a little open square. It had grass and three fruit trees, so we rested there.

'Towards sunset I began to think about our situation. Night was getting closer and my safe hiding place still had to be found. But that worried me very little now. I had with me, perhaps, the best of all defences against the Morlocks – I had matches. I had the candles in my pocket too, if more light were needed.

'It seemed to me that we should spend the night in the open, protected by a fire. In the morning I could try to get the Time Machine. To do that, at that time, I had only my metal bar. But now, with my growing knowledge, I felt very differently about those metal panels. I had never thought they were very strong, and I hoped that the metal bar would be heavy enough to do the job.

## Chapter 12   Fear of Fire

'When we came out of the palace, the sun hadn't completely gone down. I wanted to get through the woods before it was dark, and to reach the white sphinx early the next morning. My plan was to go as far as possible that night and then build a fire and sleep in the protection of its light. So as we went along I collected sticks and dry grass, and soon had my arms full.

'Because of this, we walked more slowly than I had expected, and also Weena was tired. And I began to suffer from sleepiness too, so it was night before we reached the wood. On a bushy hill at the edge of it, Weena wanted to stop, afraid of the darkness in front of us. But a strong feeling of danger, that I failed to see as a warning, made me continue. I had been without sleep for a night and two days, and felt ill and bad-tempered. I felt sleep coming on me, and the Morlocks with it.

'Then, among the black bushes behind us, and dark against their blackness, I saw three figures close to the ground. There was long grass all around us and I didn't feel safe from them. The forest, I thought, was about a kilometre across. If we could get through it to the open hillside, that, it seemed to me, was a much safer resting-place.

'I thought that with my matches and my candles I could keep my way lit through the woods. But I knew that I wouldn't be able to hold my firewood too. So, rather unwillingly, I put it down. Then it came into my head that I would surprise the Morlocks behind us by lighting it. I soon discovered how stupid this was, but at the time it seemed a good way of protecting our backs.

'I don't know if you have ever thought what an unusual thing fire must be where there are no people and where the climate is cool. The sun's heat is not often strong enough to burn plants, even when it shines through a drop of water, as sometimes happens in hotter places. Lightning may start small fires, but they don't usually spread very far. In this future time, the way to make fire had been forgotten in the world. The red tongues climbing my pile of wood were completely new and strange to Weena.

'She wanted to run to them and play with them. She almost threw herself on the fire, but I held her back. Then I picked her up and, although she fought against me, I walked forwards into the wood. For a short distance the light from my fire showed us the way. Looking back, I could see, through the many trees, that from my pile of sticks the fire had spread to some bushes. Now a curved red line was coming slowly up the grass of the hill.

'I laughed at that, and turned again to the dark trees in front of us. It was very black and Weena held on to me in fear, but there was still, as my eyes got used to the darkness, enough light for me to walk around the trees. Above us it was simply black, except where a piece of blue sky shone down on us here and there. I struck none of my matches because I had no hand free. With my left arm I carried my little friend; in my right hand I had my metal bar.

'For some time I heard nothing except the breaking of dry wood under my feet, the low sound of the wind above, my own breathing and the beat of my heart. Then I seemed to hear soft footsteps around me. I kept moving. The footsteps grew louder and then I heard the same strange sounds and voices I had heard in the Under-world. There seemed to be several of the Morlocks and they were getting closer. In fact, in another minute I felt one of them pull at my coat, then something on my arm. Weena shook violently and then stopped moving.

'It was time for a match. But to get one I had to put her down. I did so and, as I searched in my pocket, a fight began in the darkness around my knees, with no sounds from her and some strange bird-like noises from the Morlocks. Soft little hands, too, were moving over my coat and back, even touching my neck. Then the match caught fire and I saw the white backs of the Morlocks running away through the trees. I quickly took a candle from my pocket and prepared to light it.

'Then I looked at Weena. She was lying with her face to the ground, holding my feet and not moving. With a sudden feeling of fear I bent down to her. She seemed almost unable to breathe. I lit the candle and placed it on the ground, and as the flame grew it chased away the Morlocks and the shadows. I bent down and lifted her. The wood behind us seemed full of the movement and voices of the Morlocks.

'She seemed to have fainted. I put her carefully on my shoulder and stood up, and then there came a horrible thought. While lighting my match and helping Weena, I had turned myself around several times and now I had no idea which direction to go in. I might be facing back towards the Green Palace.

'Now I was cold with fear. I had to think quickly what to do. I decided to build a fire and stay where we were. I put Weena, still not moving, down against a tree. Very quickly, because my candle was burning low, I began collecting sticks and leaves. Here and there, out of the darkness around me, the Morlocks' eyes shone like jewels.

'The candle burned down and went out. I lit a match and as I did so, I saw two white shapes that were moving towards Weena. When the light shone, they ran quickly to get away. One was so blinded by the light that he came straight towards me and I felt a bone break when I hit him with my hand. He cried out in pain, walked with difficulty for a short distance and fell down. I lit another candle and continued building my fire.

'After some time, I noticed how dry some of the leaves were above me; since my arrival a week before, no rain had fallen. So instead of looking around among the trees for fallen sticks, I began jumping up and pulling down branches. Very soon I had a smoky fire of green wood and dry sticks, and could put out my candle. Then I turned to the place where Weena sat beside my metal bar. I did what I could to make her wake up, but she seemed almost dead. I couldn't even decide whether or not she was breathing.

'Now the smoke of the fire surrounded me and suddenly I felt terribly tired. My fire wouldn't need any more wood for an hour or two, so I sat down. The wood was full of quiet noises that I

*I saw two white shapes that were moving towards Weena.*

couldn't understand. I seemed just to close my eyes for a minute. But then everything was dark and the Morlocks had their hands on me.

'Throwing off their fingers, I quickly felt in my pocket for the matchbox and – it had gone! Then they took hold of me again. In a moment I realised what had happened. I had slept and my fire had gone out. I felt the fear of death. The forest seemed full of the smell of burning wood. I was caught by the neck, by the hair, by the arms, and pulled down. It was unbelievably horrible in the darkness to feel all these soft creatures lying on top of me. There were too many of them, and I fell to the ground.

'I felt little teeth biting at my neck. I turned over and as I did so, my hand touched my metal bar. It gave me strength. I fought hard to get back on my feet, shaking off the human rats. Holding the bar against my body, I pushed where I thought their faces might be. I could feel the softness of bodies and my hits, and for a moment I was free.

'I felt the strange happiness that so often seems to come with hard fighting. I knew that both I and Weena were finished, but I decided to make the Morlocks pay for their meat. I stood with my back to a tree, moving the metal bar from side to side in front of me.

'The whole wood was full of the movement and cries of the Morlocks. A minute passed. Their voices seemed to rise to a greater level of excitement and their movements grew faster. But no more came within reach. I stood staring into the blackness.

'Then suddenly hope came. Were the Morlocks afraid? And soon after that, I noticed a strange thing. The darkness seemed to grow lighter. I began to see the Morlocks around me – three half-dead at my feet. Then I recognised, with great surprise, that the others were running from behind me and away through the wood in front. And their backs seemed no longer white, but reddish.

'As I stood there, my mouth open in surprise, I saw a little cloud of smoke move across a small area of starlight between the branches and disappear. And then I understood the smell of burning wood and the quiet voices growing now into a great noise. I understood the smoke and the reason for the Morlocks' speed.

'Stepping out from behind my tree and looking back, I saw, through the nearer trees, the flames of the burning forest. It was my first fire coming after me. I looked for Weena, but she was gone. The sounds of the fire behind me, the crashing noise as each new tree caught fire, left little time to think. With my metal bar still in my hand, I followed in the Morlocks' path.

'It was a hard race. Once the flames moved forwards so quickly on my right as I ran that they got ahead of me and I had to move away to my left. But at last I came out of the trees into a small open space, and as I did so, a Morlock rushed towards me. He ran blindly past me and straight into the fire!

'And then I saw the most strange and horrible thing, I think, of all that I saw in that future age. This whole space was as bright as day with the light of the fire. In the centre was a small hill, surrounded by burned bushes. Beyond that was another arm of the burning forest, with yellow tongues of flame already coming from it, completely surrounding the space with a ring of fire. On the hillside were thirty or forty Morlocks, blinded by the light and the heat, running here and there against each other in their fear.

'At first I didn't understand their blindness and struck angrily at them with my bar, in terror, as they came close to me. I killed one and hurt another. But when I had watched the movements of one of them under the bushes against the red sky, and heard their cries, I understood their total helplessness and pain in the strong light and I hit no more of them.

'But now and then one ran straight towards me, frightening

me so much that I got out of his way. At one time the flames became a little less bright and I was afraid the awful creatures would be able to see me. I was even thinking of beginning the fight by killing some of them before this happened, but the fire started up again and I stopped myself. I walked around the hill among them and kept out of their way, looking for a sign of Weena. But Weena was gone.

'At last I sat down on the top of the little hill and watched this strange group of blind creatures feeling their way here and there. They made inhuman noises to each other, as the heat from the fire affected them. The smoke rushed up and blew across the sky, and through the occasional spaces in it, the little stars shone. Two or three Morlocks ran into me and I fought them off with my hands, shaking as I did so.

'For most of that night I felt that I was having a bad dream. I bit myself and screamed to make myself wake up. I hit the ground with my hands and got up and sat down again. I walked around, and again sat down. Then I started calling to God to let me wake.

'Three times I saw Morlocks put their heads down in great pain and rush into the flames. But at last, above the dying red of the fire, above the great clouds of black smoke and the whitening and blackening trees, and the decreasing numbers of Morlocks, came the white light of the day.

'I looked again for signs of Weena, but there were none. It was clear that they had left her poor little body in the burning forest. I can't describe how glad I was that it hadn't been eaten. As I thought of that, I wanted to kill the helpless Morlocks around me, but I managed to control myself.

'The hill, as I have said, was a kind of island in the forest. From the top of it, I could now see the Green Palace through the thin smoke, and from that I could work out my direction to the white sphinx. And so, leaving the last of the Morlocks running and crying, I tied some grass around my feet and limped across smoking grass and burnt wood, still hot inside, towards the hiding-place of the Time Machine.

'I walked slowly, because I was very tired and my feet were painful. I was so sorry about the death of little Weena. It seemed such a terrible thing. Now, back in my own room, it feels more like the sadness of a dream than a real sadness. But that morning I felt very lonely again – terribly alone. I began to think of this house, of this fireside, of some of you, and with these thoughts came a great need to return.

'But as I walked over the smoking ground under the bright morning sky, I made a discovery. In my trouser pocket there were still some loose matches. The box had broken open before it was lost.

## Chapter 13    A Fight for the Time Machine

'At about eight or nine in the morning I came to the same seat of yellow metal from which I had looked at the world on the evening of my arrival. I thought of my first ideas about this future world on that evening, and I couldn't stop myself laughing at my confidence.

'I was sad to think how short the dream of human intelligence had been. It had tried to make a comfortable, fair and safe society. It had succeeded – and had then led to this. We forget the law of nature – that change, danger and trouble make us think harder. Nature never asks the brain to work until habit and feeling are useless. There is no intelligence where there is no change and no need of change.

'So as I see it, the Upper-world people had moved towards their weak prettiness, and the Under-world to hard work. But it seemed that as time passed, the Upper-world had stopped feeding the Under-world. And when other meat failed them, the people of the Under-world had started to eat what hadn't been allowed before. That is how I understood the situation in my last view of the world of 802,701.

'Although I was unhappy, this seat, the peaceful view and the warm sunlight were very pleasant after the hard work, excitement and terror of the past few days. I was very tired and sleepy, and so I spread myself out on the grass and slept.

'I woke up a little before sunset and, stretching myself, I walked down the hill towards the white sphinx. And now a most unexpected thing happened. As I came to the pedestal, I found that the metal doors were open. I stopped in front of them, not sure about entering. Inside was a small room, and on a higher place in the corner of this was the Time Machine. I had the small levers in my pocket. So here, after all my thought about breaking in, was an easy solution. I threw my metal bar away, almost sorry not to use it.

'A sudden thought came into my head as I bent towards the door. This time, at least, I understood the thinking of the Morlocks. Trying not to laugh, I stepped through the door and up to the Time Machine. I was surprised to find it had been carefully oiled and cleaned. I have thought since then that the Morlocks had even partly taken it to pieces while trying in their slow way to understand it.

'Now as I stood and examined it, finding pleasure in just touching it, it happened. I had expected it. The metal panels suddenly closed with a loud noise. I was in the dark and couldn't get out. This is what the Morlocks thought, I was certain. I smiled.

'I could already hear them laughing softly as they came towards me. Very calmly I tried to strike a match. I only had to fix the levers and leave then like a ghost. But I had forgotten one little thing. Those matches could only be lit by striking them against the box.

'You can imagine how all my calm disappeared. The little creatures were close to me. One touched me. I struck at them with the levers and began to get into the seat of the machine. Then one hand touched me and then another. After that I simply had to fight against their fingers for my levers and at the same time feel for the places where these fitted.

'One lever, in fact, almost got away from me. As it left my hand, I had to hit in the dark with my head – I could hear the Morlock's head ring – to get it back. This was an even more dangerous fight than the fight in the forest, I think.

'But at last the lever was fixed and I pulled it. The little hands fell away from me. The darkness soon changed to the same grey light that I have already described.

## Chapter 14   The Death of the World

'I have already told you of the sickness and confusion that comes with time travelling. And this time I wasn't sitting safely in the seat. For some time I held onto the machine as it moved from side to side, not thinking about my journey.

'When I looked at the dials again I was very surprised to find where I had arrived. One dial shows days, another thousands of days, another millions of days, and another thousands of millions. Instead of pushing the levers backwards, I had pulled them forwards, and when I looked at the dials I found that the thousands hand was moving round as fast as the seconds hand of a watch – into the future.

'As I continued travelling, the appearance of things changed in a strange way. First the greyness grew darker. Then the times of each day and night grew longer and longer. At first this seemed strange because I was still travelling at high speed. But then I understood that the world had slowed down, and now each movement of the sun across the sky lasted for years.

'At last an unchanging half-light covered the world. The sun's line of light had disappeared, because it simply came up and went down in the west and grew wider and redder. The moon had totally disappeared. The movement of the stars had grown slower and slower. Finally, some time before I stopped, a large, red sun stopped moving. At one time it had become brighter for a short time, but it quickly lost its light again.

'I understood that the Earth had stopped turning and was resting with one side facing the sun, just as in our own time the moon faces the Earth. Very nervously, because I remembered my first fall, I began to slow the machine down. The hands on the dials moved slower and slower until the thousands dial seemed to stop and the daily one could be seen again. I slowed down more, until I could begin to see an empty beach.

'I stopped very gently and sat in the Time Machine, looking round. The sky was no longer blue. To the north-east it was inky black, and out of the darkness the pale white stars shone clearly and brightly. Overhead it was deep red and starless, and to the south-east it grew brighter to the point where half of the sun could be seen above the line of the land. The rocks around me were of a dull reddish colour. Some very green plants covered every part of their south-eastern side, and these were the only living things that I could see.

'The machine was standing on a beach. The sea was to the south-west. There were no waves, because there was no wind. The sea moved very slowly up and down like gentle breathing. And along the edge of the water was a thick line of salt – pink against the brightly-coloured sky. I noticed that I was breathing very fast. This reminded me of my only experience of climbing mountains, and I knew that the air was thinner than it is now.

'Far away up the empty beach I heard a scream and saw a thing like an enormous insect go flying up into the sky. It circled and disappeared over some low hills beyond. The sound of its voice was so sad that I shook and sat myself more safely on the machine.

'Looking round me again, I saw that, quite near, a large red rock – I had thought it was a rock – was moving slowly towards me. Then I saw that the thing was really a large crab-like creature. Can you imagine a crab as large as that table, with its many legs moving slowly and uncertainly and its eyes looking at you?

'As I stared at this horrible creature, I felt something on my face. I tried to brush it away with my hand, but in a moment it returned and almost immediately I felt another by my ear. I struck at this and found something like a long string. It was pulled quickly out of my hand. With a great feeling of fear, I turned and saw that another enormous crab was standing just behind me. Its horrible eyes were moving, its mouth was open with hunger and it was going to attack me.

'In a moment my hand was on the lever and I had put a month between myself and these creatures. But I was still on the same beach and I saw them clearly now when I stopped. Large numbers of them seemed to be moving here and there, in the dull light, among the strong green plants.

'I can't make you understand the feeling of great emptiness that hung over the world. The red eastern sky, the darkness to the north, the salt Dead Sea, the thin air, all had a horrible effect. I moved a hundred years further into the future, and there was the same red sun – a little larger, a little darker – the same dying sea, the same cold air, and the same crowd of crabs moving slowly in and out of the green plants and the red rocks. And in the west I saw a curved pale line like a large new moon.

'So I travelled, stopping now and again, in great steps of a thousand years or more, wanting to know what happened to the Earth. I watched, with a strange interest, the sun grow larger and duller in the western sky, and the life of the old Earth die away. At last, more than thirty million years from

*Another enormous crab was standing just behind me.*

now, the enormous red sun covered almost a tenth of the darkening sky.

'Then I stopped again and the hundreds of crabs had disappeared. Now the red beach, except for its green plants, seemed lifeless. A strong cold attacked me and snow fell from time to time. There was ice along the edge of the sea, with large pieces further out, but most of that salt ocean – all bloody under the sky – was still unfrozen.

'I looked around me to see if any animals were still alive, but I saw nothing moving, on the land or in the sky or sea. A low island of sand had appeared in the sea and the water had moved back from the beach. I thought I saw a black object moving around on this, but it stopped moving when I looked at it, and I decided that it was just a rock. The stars in the sky were very bright.

'Suddenly I noticed that the shape of the sun in the west had changed and that something was moving into its circle. For a minute, perhaps, I stared in shock at this and then I realised that either the moon or Mercury was passing across the sun.

'It became darker and darker, a cold wind began to blow from the east and the snow fell more and more heavily. Except for these lifeless sounds the world was silent. Silent? It would be hard to describe the quietness of it all. All the everyday sounds of people, and of sheep, birds and insects – all that had ended. As the darkness grew, the snow fell more heavily and it turned colder. The soft wind grew stronger. In another moment only the pale stars could be seen. Everything else was darkness. The sky was completely black.

'This great darkness was horrible to me. I shook, and began to feel very sick. Then, like a red-hot curve in the sky, the edge of the sun appeared. I got off the machine to recover. I felt unable to face the return journey. As I stood there, I saw again the moving thing on the island – there was no mistake now that it was a moving thing – against the red water of the sea. It was round, the size of a football perhaps, and long arms hung down from it.

'Then I felt that I was fainting. But a terrible fear of lying helpless in that awful half-darkness gave me strength while I climbed back into the seat.

## Chapter 15   Coming Home

'So I came back. I think I fainted in the machine. When I felt better the change from day to night had started again, the sun was golden and the sky was blue. I breathed more freely. The shape of the land moved here and there. At last I saw again the shadows of houses, the signs of humans. These, too, changed and passed, and others came. Soon I began to recognise our own smaller and familiar buildings, and the hand of the thousands dial returned to its starting point. Then the old walls of the laboratory came round me. Very gently now, I slowed the machine down.

'I think I have told you that when I started, before my speed became very high, Mrs Watchett, my cook, had walked across the room. She moved, as it seemed to me, very quickly. As I returned, I passed again across that minute and now all her movements appeared to be the exact opposite of the ones she had made before. And just before that, I seemed to see you, Hillyer, for a moment.'

The Time Traveller looked at me as he spoke.

'Then I stopped the machine, got off it very shakily and sat down on my chair. For several minutes I shook violently. Then I became calmer. Around me was my old laboratory again, exactly as it had been. But not exactly! The machine had started from the south-east corner. It had stopped again in the north-west. This gives you the exact distance from my little lawn to the pedestal of the white sphinx into which the Morlocks had carried it.

'For a time my brain went dead. Then I got up and came through here, limping because my heel was still painful. I saw the newspaper on the table by the door. I found the date really was today and, looking at the clock, I saw that the time was almost eight o'clock. I heard your voices and the sound of plates. I smelled well-cooked meat and opened the door to the dining-room. You know the rest.'

He looked at the Medical Man.

'No. I can't expect you to believe it. Accept it as a lie – or as a guess at the future. Say I dreamed it in the laboratory. But as a story, what do you think of it?'

He picked up his pipe and began, in his usual way, to play with it in his hands. I took my eyes off his face and looked around at the others. The Medical Man was staring at our host. The Editor was looking hard at the end of his cigarette – his sixth. The Journalist searched in his pocket for his watch. The others, as I remember, did not move.

The Editor stood up and shook his head. 'What a pity that you are not a writer of stories!' he said, putting his hand on the Time Traveller's shoulder.

'You don't believe it?'

'Well –'

'I thought not.'

The Time Traveller turned to us. 'Where are the matches?' he said. He lit his pipe, blowing smoke. 'To tell you the truth, I can't really believe it myself . . . But . . .'

His eye fell with a questioning look on the dead white flowers on the little table. Then he turned over the hand holding his pipe. I saw he was looking at some red marks.

The Medical Man rose, came to the lamp and examined the flowers. 'This one is odd,' he said. The Psychologist bent forwards to see, holding out his hand for one of them. 'It's strange,' said the Medical Man, 'but I certainly don't know what type of flowers these are. Can I have them?'

The Time Traveller thought for a few seconds. Then he suddenly said, 'Certainly not.'

'Where did you really get them?' said the Medical Man.

The Time Traveller put his hand to his head. I thought he was trying to remember something. 'They were put into my pocket by Weena.' He stared round the room. 'I'm beginning to forget it all. Did I ever make a Time Machine, or a model of a Time Machine? Or is it only a dream? I must look at that machine. If there *is* one!'

He picked up the lamp quickly and carried it through the door. We followed him. There in the lamplight was the machine, with brown spots and mud on it, bits of grass on the lower parts and one side bent.

The Time Traveller put the lamp down on the table and touched the damaged side. 'It's all right now,' he said. 'My story was true. I am sorry I brought you out here in the cold.' He picked up the lamp and in total silence we returned to the smoking room.

He came into the hall with us and helped the Editor on with his coat. The Medical Man looked into his face and, after a few seconds, told him he was suffering from too much work. The Time Traveller laughed loudly. I remember him standing at the open door, shouting good night.

I walked some distance with the Editor. He thought the story was 'a colourful lie'. I was unable to make up my mind. It was so strange, and the telling was so believable and serious. I lay awake most of the night thinking about it.

The next day, I went to see the Time Traveller again. I was told he was in the laboratory. I went there but it was empty.

I stared for a minute at the Time Machine and put out a hand

and touched the lever. It shook like a branch in the wind. Its movements surprised me greatly, and I had a strange memory of childhood days, when I was not allowed to touch things. I went back into the smoking room and found the Time Traveller there. He had a small camera under one arm and a bag under the other. He laughed when he saw me. 'I'm very busy,' he said, 'with that thing in there.'

'But is it not a joke?' I said. 'Do you really travel through time?'

'Really and truly I do.' And he looked straight into my eyes. 'I only want half an hour,' he said. 'I know why you came and it is very good of you. There are some magazines here. If you will stay for lunch I shall prove this time-travelling to you completely. I shall even bring back some things for you to look at. Will you forgive me if I leave you now?'

I agreed, not really understanding the full meaning of his words, and he left the room. I heard the door of the laboratory shut, sat down in a chair and picked up the daily paper. What was he going to do before lunch-time? Then suddenly I was reminded by an advertisement that I had promised to meet a friend at two. I looked at my watch and saw that there was just enough time. I got up and went to tell the Time Traveller.

As I took hold of the handle of the laboratory door I heard a shout, then strange noises. A sudden wind blew round me as I opened the door, and from inside came the sound of broken glass falling on the floor. The Time Traveller was not there. I seemed to see a ghostly, unclear figure sitting in a moving machine for a moment, but all of this disappeared. The Time Machine had gone. The window was broken.

I was surprised and unable to understand. As I stood staring, the door into the garden opened and a servant appeared.

We looked at each other. Then ideas began to come. 'Has Mr _____ gone out that way?' I said.

'No, sir. No one has come out this way.'

And then I understood. I stayed there, waiting for the Time Traveller; waiting for the second, perhaps stranger story, and the objects and photographs he would bring with him. But I am beginning to fear that I must wait a lifetime. The Time Traveller disappeared three years ago. And as everyone knows now, he has never returned.

# ACTIVITIES

## Chapters 1–3

*Before you read*

1 In this book, the Time Traveller goes into the distant future. If you had the chance to travel in time, would you choose to visit the near future, the distant future or the past? If you chose the future, what changes would you hope to see? If you chose the past, what time in history would you like to visit? Discuss your ideas.

2 Look at the Word List at the back of this book. Which two words are words for:
   a people's jobs?
   b parts of a machine?
   c green living things?

*While you read*

3 When the Time Traveller explains his ideas, his guests argue with him. Which of these reasons do they give to say that time travel is impossible? Tick (✓) them.

   a We can't move in time like we can move in space.      .....

   b You can't travel into the past because you might change history.      .....

   c If something travels into the future, you can still see it, because it has to travel through the present.      .....

4 Which of these people attend both dinners at the Time Traveller's house? Tick (✓) them.

   a journalist      .....

   a very young man      .....

   the Medical Man      .....

   a quiet shy man with a beard      .....

   Filby      .....

   the Editor      .....

   the Psychologist      .....

*After you read*

5 Which of these things does the Time Traveller *not* believe?
   a We can travel completely freely in space.
   b Mathematical models are only ideas.
   c All real things must exist in time.
   d You can't see an object which is travelling quickly in time.

6 HG Wells' character, the Time Traveller, is a man who is rich enough to live in a large house. Most of his friends seem to be in good jobs. Think about modern books or films about time travel. In what ways are the time travellers different?

7 At the end of Chapter 3, the Time Traveller meets the first of the people of the future. He is small, thin and weak, and seems very beautiful. How surprised are you by this? How do you think human beings will change over the next few hundred thousand years? Why?

**Chapters 4–6**

*Before you read*

8 A number of things might happen to the Time Traveller when he meets the people of the future. Which of these do you think is most likely?
   a They will catch him and try to kill him.
   b They will think he is a god, and make him their leader.
   c They are much more intelligent and will think of him as an interesting pet.
   d Other humans are attacking them and he will help them.

9 *The Time Machine* first appeared, as a book, in 1895. Which of these modern inventions do you think the writer could imagine, and includes in the story:

aeroplanes   computers   modern weapons   space travel
supermarkets   television   very tall buildings

**10** Number these events in the correct order, from 1 to 8.

    **a** The Time Traveller eats fruit with the people.     . . . . .

    **b** He hits a metal panel with a stone.     . . . . .

    **c** He tries to learn a new language.     . . . . .

    **d** He wakes up some of the people.     . . . . .

    **e** He takes the levers from his machine.     . . . . .

    **f** The people throw flowers over him.     . . . . .

    **g** He finds strange narrow footprints in the grass.     . . . . .

    **h** He climbs to the top of a hill.     . . . . .

    **i** The Time Machine disappears.     . . . . .

*After you read*

**11** Why does the Time Traveller think the people of the future have become physically weak?

    **a** Because they only eat fruit.

    **b** Because they don't have to work.

    **c** Because their lives are easy.

**12** Imagine you are the Time Traveller and have arrived in the year 802,701. Which of these would you be most and least interested in? Make your choices and then discuss them with someone who has made different choices.

    **a** how people live together

    **b** how their society is organised

    **c** the new inventions they use

    **d** their history, since your time

    **e** how much money you could make

    **f** relationships you might have with them

    **g** learning their language

**13** You arrive in the year 802,701 and a small group of people walk towards you. There are a number of things you might do. You could walk forwards and try to make friends with them; wait to see what they will do; run away, or look around for a weapon. With another student, discuss what you would do and why.

## Chapters 7–9

*Before you read*

**14** Who do you think has taken the Time Machine?

    **a** The people who live in the large building.

    **b** Another group of similar people who live not far away.

    **c** Some less pleasant people who live underground.

    **d** Creatures from another world.

    Think about how each of these could change the story. Now discuss your ideas with another student.

**15** In Chapter 9 the Time Traveller says he has travelled into the future without weapons, medicine, a camera or even enough matches. Choose four of these things to take with you on a trip into the future:

    a book   a camera   a change of clothes   a daily newspaper
    a gun   a map   a radio   an electric torch   medicine

    Now add two more things that are your own choice. Explain your choices.

*While you read*

**16** Decide whether these sentences are true (T) or false (F).

    **a** The Time Traveller doesn't want to walk far from the large building because he is worried about his machine. . . . . .

    **b** He saves Weena's life by swimming after her. . . . . .

    **c** On the night before he saves Weena, he sees a white creature in his room. . . . . .

    **d** He doesn't climb down the well at first because he was afraid. . . . . .

    **e** He quite quickly understands that the white creatures are also human. . . . . .

    **f** He climbs down the well to get to the Time Machine. . . . . .

    **g** He realises that the Morlocks eat meat. . . . . .

*After you read*

**17** The Time Traveller realises that a second type of people live underground. Put these reasons in the order that they happen in the story.

    **a** He sees white figures on the hillside.

    **b** He chases a white creature down a well.

    **c** He discovers that air goes down into the wells.

    **d** He hears sounds like big engines from the wells.

    **e** The Eloi sleep in groups because they are afraid.

    **f** The Eloi wear clothes and shoes but don't make them.

**18** The Time Traveller compares the society of his own time with a society of the future. Which of these have already come true in your country?

    **a** The differences between workers and managers have increased.

    **b** Marriage between the social classes has become less and less frequent.

    **c** People live and work more and more underground.

**19** The Morlocks are the workers in this future world. They live underground and are horrible and violent. What does this tell us of Wells's ideas about the society of his time? Discuss your ideas with another student.

## Chapters 10–12

*Before you read*

**20** The Time Traveller visits a ruined museum containing many things from the past. Choose ten objects from our time which you would like people in the distant future to see. Discuss your choices with another student.

**21** In the next part of the book, the Time Traveller looks for a place to live where he can be safe from the Morlocks. Think what you might do in his situation.

**22** Which of these things does the Time Traveller see in the Green Palace? Tick (✓) them.

| | | | |
|---|---|---|---|
| an electric torch | ..... | animal bones | ..... |
| birds' eggs | ..... | books | ..... |
| candles | ..... | clocks | ..... |
| clothes | ..... | glass cases | ..... |
| guns | ..... | knives | ..... |
| machines | ..... | magazines | ..... |
| matches | ..... | rocks | ..... |
| tinned food | ..... | glass balls | ..... |

*After you read*

**23** The Time Traveller has four reasons for going to the Green Palace. These are:

**a** To find a safe place to live.

**b** To make or find a weapon.

**c** To find a way of making fire.

**d** To find a way of breaking open the metal panels.

Which of these does he manage to do successfully?

**24** 'I looked again for signs of Weena, but there were none.' Why do you think HG Wells arranges for Weena to disappear from the story?

**a** To make his readers feel sad.

**b** To make it easier for the Time Traveller to return to his own time.

**c** Because he didn't want the book to become a love story.

Discuss your opinions with another student.

## Chapters 13–15

*Before you read*

**25** Which of these do you think will happen in the next three chapters?

**a** The Time Traveller goes back down the well and finds his Time Machine.

**b**  The panels on the pedestal open and he finds his Time Machine inside.

   **c**  He finds that the Eloi have taken his machine and destroyed it.

   **d**  He realises that he will never find his machine and decides to stay in the future.

*While you read*

**26**  Which of these happen in Chapters 13–15? Write a tick (✓) or a cross (✗).

   **a**  The Time Traveller climbs to the top of the hill again.           .....

   **b**  He opens a panel and gets inside the pedestal.           .....

   **c**  He finds the Time Machine inside the pedestal.           .....

   **d**  The Morlocks destroy the Time Machine.           .....

   **e**  The Time Traveller is surprised when the panel on the pedestal suddenly closes.           .....

   **f**  He strikes a match and the Morlocks run away.           .....

   **g**  He escapes the Morlocks by travelling further into the future.           .....

   **h**  He stops on a beach and is attacked by three enormous crabs.           .....

   **i**  He finally arrives more than thirty million years into the future.           .....

   **j**  There are no living things in the world at this time.           .....

   **k**  He comes home and tells his story but nobody believes him.           .....

   **l**  He leaves his home on a second visit to the future and returns after three years.           .....

*After you read*

**27**  When he escapes from the Morlocks inside the pedestal, the Time Traveller goes into the future and stops the machine on a beach. Which of these statements about the world of that time are true?

   **a**  The world is now turning very slowly.

   **b**  There is no wind.

   **c**  There is ice along the edge of the sea.

   **d**  The air is thinner.

**e** The plants are a strong green colour.

**f** The only moving things are crabs.

**g** The rocks are a dull reddish colour.

**28** Work with another student. Act out a conversation between the Editor and the Medical Man a year after the Time Traveller disappears again.

*Student A*: You are the Editor. You still don't believe the Time Traveller's story.

*Student B*: You are the Medical Man. After seeing the flowers, you weren't so sure. Since the Time Traveller's disappearance, you are even less certain.

## Writing

**29** Think about the ways of life of the Eloi and the Morlocks. Think about what they eat and what they do with their time. Which would you prefer to be – an Eloi or a Morlock? Explain your preference in writing.

**30** Imagine that you are a time traveller. You have gone fifty years into the future but now your machine is broken and you can't go back. Also, you feel that you may not live much longer. Write a letter for your friends to find fifty years later. Describe the changes in the world of the future and how you feel about them.

**31** If you could choose to travel back in time, which year would you choose? Which historical event would you like to see? Write about a time, a place and an event, and why you would like to be there.

**32** Write another short chapter for the book. Imagine the Time Traveller has gone away for three years, and then returned, bringing Weena with him. He invites his friends to dinner again and tells them about his experience. Write the story of what happened in his second visit to the future.

**33** Think about a time in your life when you made the wrong decision or a mistake, or did something you were sorry about later. Write letter to a friend who was there. Explain what you would do differently if you had a second chance.

**34** In Chapter 1 the Time Traveller explains his ideas, in Chapter 2 he returns from his travels and then in Chapter 3 he begins to tell his story. Do you think that this is a good way to put the book together? For example, would it be better if Chapter 2 came at the end? Give reasons for your answer.

**35** HG Wells describes a time machine that is open, with a seat and some levers and dials. It is very much a machine of his time. Write a description of what a modern machine might look like.

**36** 'If you travelled back in time you might, for example, kill someone in your own family, with the result that you would not be born. For reasons like this, time travel is not possible.' Give your opinion on this.

**37** People in many countries today are taller than they were a hundred years ago, not because they have to be but because they eat better food. Do you think they will continue to grow bigger or will they stop growing? Write your ideas about physical changes to people in the next hundred years.

**38** Imagine that someone from 100 years ago has travelled forwards in time. Write a conversation with them in which you explain the changes in the world and how to live in the world of today.

# WORD LIST

**bush** (n) a plant like a small tree with a lot of branches

**candle** (n) a stick that produces light when it burns

**comfort** (n) a feeling of being physically relaxed and satisfied

**crab** (n) a sea animal with ten legs, which you can find on the beach

**creature** (n) an animal, fish or insect

**dial** (n) a round part of a machine with numbers showing measurements

**dimension** (n) a size of something, like its length, width or height

**editor** (n) a person who decides what is included in a newspaper

**experiment** (n) a scientific test which you do to find out or prove something

**geometry** (n) the study in mathematics of the form and relationships of lines, curves and shapes

**laboratory** (n) a room where a scientist does tests

**lawn** (n) an area of grass that is cut short

**lever** (n) a handle on a machine that you move to work the machine

**limp** (n/v) a way of walking with difficulty because one leg is hurt

**museum** (n) a building containing important things from science and history

**object** (n) a thing that you can see, hold or touch

**panel** (n) a flat piece of metal or wood that is part of a door or wall

**pedestal** (n) a large piece of stone on which a stone or metal figure stands

**psychologist** (n) someone who studies the human mind

**recover** (n) to get better after being hurt or shocked

**reflect** (v) to show a picture of something in a mirror or water

**rise** (n) to increase, go up or stand up

**robe** (n) a long, loose piece of clothing that people wear

**species** (n) a group of animals or plants of the same kind

**sphinx** (n) an old Egyptian figure like a large cat with a human head

**torch** (n) a long stick that you burn at one end for light

**truth** (n) the true facts about something

**tunnel** (n) a long hole through the ground or a mountain

**weapon** (n) something like a knife or gun, used for fighting

**well** (n) a deep hole in the ground from which water is taken